My Summer With The Senator
By T.S. Dawson

Acknowledgements

Thank you so much for giving your time to my writing. I hope you enjoy reading this book as much as I enjoyed writing it.

As always, thank you to Wesley and Terry, my son and husband, for all of your love and support. I am so glad you all continue to tolerate me when I am suffering from writer's block or frustrated because my "real job" won't let me mentally commit to my dream job, writing.

I know this is repetitive, but to the T.S. Dawson team, Donna Goss, Christie Hartley Johnson, John Bryan and Annette Saunders, thank you so much for all of your help. I really could not do this without your editing, critique and computer skills and for being my sounding boards. I'm sorry if I hound you all over my self-imposed deadlines. Thank you for all that you do for me and the characters in the books.

As always, thank you to the stores that carry my books, Genuine Georgia in Greensboro, Georgia, The Bookworm in Louisville, Georgia, The Paisley Bag in Wrens, Georgia and The Georgia College and State University Bookstore.

Thank you to all of the bloggers and Facebook page operators that help us Indie authors get the word out about our books. Thank you to those who promote and those who review.

Thank you Molly Phipps for the most awesome book cover ever!

Thank you all from the bottom of my heart and please enjoy my latest work and tell your friends and, please, don't forget to leave a review. I love hearing from you and a review is a great way to let me and other readers what I did well or what I need to do to improve.

Sincerely,
T.S. Dawson

My Summer With The Senator

Chapter 1

I took my coffee black and I took it on the side porch overlooking the meadow and the creek. Kicked back in one of the rocking chairs with the morning paper, that's how I started every morning at work. This was the life, my life.

I was the Inn Manager and Director of Sales at Seven Springs. Seven Springs was a hotel built around the turn of the 20th century as a stop on the railroad between Louisville, Georgia, the former capital, and Atlanta, what folks around rural Jefferson County still called the "new capital." It was bursting with history and I loved it.

I was fortunate my friend Millie, whom I'd met during my failed attempt at law school, owned Seven Springs. Millie and I met during my first year at Mercer. She was struggling with school and family life. I was struggling with a broken heart. Our struggles were vastly different, but we bonded over them anyway when she was assigned as my student advisor.

Millie was the modern day patron saint of lost causes. When I was at my worst, she saved me much like she'd saved this old hotel from the wrecking ball. I was my own wrecking ball and depression was the chain that swung it.

Millie's husband, Gabe, ran the restaurant and, for the most part, he was my boss. I coordinated with him on event sales like weddings and corporate outings. Although it was Millie's idea to give me a job, it was Gabe that brought me on to oversee the reconstruction of Seven Springs while Millie finished law school and he worked at another resort. In my early days, I was the middle man between them and the contractors. I was the interior decorator, gardening specialist, part-time plumber, cleaning lady and generally the jack-of-all-trades. It was a far cry from my Atlanta roots, but I felt about as proud of this old place as they did. Growing up in a neighborhood off of Paces Ferry in Atlanta, I never would have dreamed near-seclusion and the slow pace of country life was where I would find myself, but it was. Gabe and Millie gave my life purpose when I needed it most. Seven Springs was as much a part of me now as it was them.

This morning was going just like all of the other mornings had gone since the hotel opened. I was settled in to my favorite chair, sipping my coffee and waiting for Gabe. It was that spot on the porch where we had what Gabe referred to as our morning pow-wows.

This morning took a bit of a turn when I unfolded the paper and saw one of the faces occupying the front page. "Augusta National to Host Presidential Candidates" were the words splashed across the headline. Under the words were photos of the men competing not only in the upcoming charity tournament, but also the Republican nomination for President of the United States. One of the faces staring back at me was the love of my life.

In the shock of it all I bumped my coffee mug off the arm of the rocker, shattering it when it hit the floor. I screamed from the scalding coffee splashing up my legs.

"Caroline!" Gabe shouted as he ran my way. "Are you alright?" he asked while tearing off his apron and giving it to me to use as a towel. Gabe saw the entire fiasco.

"I'm fine. Just clumsy."

I truly was clumsy. I'd been that way all my life, but I wasn't okay. My leg burned, but that was the least of it. I'd found a new life here at Seven Springs and I'd finally put my broken heart in the past. At least, that's what I thought until my reaction to the picture in the paper.

"Are you sure? I'll get the first aid kit if you need it," he offered while I dabbed off and assessed the damage to my shin and calf.

My right leg suffered the brunt of it, but I hardly felt a thing. My mind was stuck on the photo. It might have been a black and white photo, but the eyes staring back at me were the prettiest shade of blue I'd ever seen. I knew them all too well.

"No, no, that's not necessary." I tried to refocus. "What's on tap for today?"

"Nothing really." Gabe took a seat in the rocking chair next me and I returned to mine as well. He opened his itinerary book and flipped to the page with today's date.

Gabe continued, "We've got the Rowland wedding this weekend so I'm going to get started on that."

I stared blankly over the railing at the stream while Gabe made notes in the binder. He was focused on work, but my mind was about five hundred miles away on the beaches of South Walton County, Florida. It was hard looking at Gabe that morning. I hope he didn't notice, but he had similar blue eyes and I didn't think I could take looking at them. Four years had passed since I saw the real thing, but I feared I might cry anyway.

"I trust all of the rooms are booked both Friday and Saturday night?" he asked.

"I'm sorry. What?" I had no idea what he'd asked.

"The rooms in the hotel, all eleven are booked for the wedding, right?"

"Oh, yes, and two of the cabins." I could have booked all twelve if I'd wanted to move out of my room for the weekend.

"Excellent! If we could get a gig like this every weekend..."

I stopped him, "You'd never see your children."

7

"That's what Mondays and Tuesdays are for," he chuckled.

It was Wednesday to most people, but this was our version of Monday. Wednesdays were generally slow and we busted our humps on Fridays, Saturdays and Sundays. Our weekends were Mondays and Tuesdays, but we typically did some sort of work those days, too.

"Luckily your wife's her own boss so she can set her hours and be off those days, too."

"Exactly!"

"Speaking of Millie, will she be in today? She doesn't have court or anything, does she?" I asked.

"I don't think so. As far as I know she should be in at any moment."

After seeing the photo in the paper I was dying to talk to Millie. She wasn't just my boss, she was one of my best friends. She's one of the few people that knew the real reason I came close to flunking out of law school before dropping out and tucking tail for home.

Gabe and I finished hashing out the plans for the Rowland wedding that weekend. Gabe wasn't one for pacing himself. He couldn't just relax on the porch and take in the scenery like Millie and I could. He always had to be busy. I was no psychologist, but in my layman's opinion, Gabe was a little OCD over the restaurant. Millie and I were not like that at all. We saw what needed to be done and did it, but we could also enjoy the view the wraparound porch afforded us. Some of our best conversations had been held on that porch.

Discussing business strategies for the hotel or life in general, it didn't matter. This was a perfect spot for it. In fact, I'd sold a great many of our events to clients while seated with them in this very chair.

With Gabe downstairs and the porch to myself, I unfolded the paper again.

"Be still my heart," I thought out loud.

Jackson Belgrave hadn't aged a day since I'd last saw him. I couldn't help myself. I skimmed the article.

This weekend. That's when he'd be playing golf in Augusta. Thirty-five miles away, that's how far he'd be from me.

I fanned myself for the perspiration that took over me every time I laid eyes on him. I shook my head as I fanned and thought about what a fool I was and what I fool I had been.

The porch was bringing me no peace this morning so I grabbed what was left of my mug and carried it and the paper inside. I dropped the paper in the first trash can I came across. I had several projects around the inn that needed tending to before the guests started arriving for the wedding on Friday. I figured there was no time like the present to get started on them.

The rest of the morning passed in a haze. I fixed a leak in one of the bathroom sinks, swapped out the winter linens on all of the beds and put on the spring and summer ones. Ordinarily there was nothing like a little hard work to clear my head. Today was not ordinary. Today nothing was clearing my mind. It just kept dwelling on the past. Dwelling and dwelling and dwelling.

"Jesus Christ!" I mumbled to myself as I fluffed the pillows in the last of the guest rooms.

I was frustrated over not being able to shake his image and dislodge it from my mind. I just couldn't un-see that photograph or forget what I read about him being in town, well, in Augusta, which was pretty dang close to being in town. I'd done so well to stop thinking of him and now here I was again. Consumed.

Jackson Belgrave was listed as the candidate from Florida. Even after all these years my poor heart still ached over him. From time to time, I still had a good cry over him and what might have been. Apparently, today was one of those days that would inevitably end in my tears. No matter how hard I tried to keep them at bay, I never succeeded.

Fearing the water works were coming, I clutched the pillow I'd been fluffing tight to my chest. I squeezed it like a childhood teddy bear as I took a seat on the side of the bed.

"Damn it!" I repeated three times.

Chapter 2

May, 1997...

"I can't believe your parents let her leave the house dressed like that," my tart of a sister-in-law remarked to my brother. She spoke as if I wasn't even in the room.

"Caroline can't help that she's built like a brick shit house," Chris joked.

"Eww!" I shivered.

I could always count on my brother, Chris, not to help defuse the situation with Becky on my behalf. I shot him a half-hearted smile even though comments about me like that were just weird coming from my brother.

"Seriously, the 'S' word in front of your daughter? Classy." Becky chastised him.

Becky then turned her attention back to me, but continued to speak directly to Chris.

"She could at least cover up a little." She snapped at him while continuing to pack Bailey's beach toys in a bag. My tiny bikini clearly offended her delicate eyes.

Bailey, their daughter, bounced around me impatiently, begging me to hurry up so we could get down to the beach. Although her mother never shielded anyone in the family from her contempt for me, that didn't keep her from sloughing Bailey off on me every chance she got.

"How's it coming with baby number two?" I asked Becky as I threw my towel over my arm and grabbed my hat.

Becky rolled her eyes in response.

Chris and Becky had been married for nine years, had Bailey within days of their first anniversary and had been trying for a second child ever since the doctors gave Becky the go ahead. The inability to get the job done was a sore spot with Becky and Chris. Becky hadn't worked a

11

day since she found out she was pregnant with Bailey and that ate at Chris. She had a hundred thousand dollar pharmacy degree from Emory and he expected her to get more use out of it than doling out ibuprofen and Benadryl to their daughter. Becky's stance was that as long as she was trying to conceive, she couldn't handle the stress of working outside of the home.

If I'd heard it once, I'd heard it a thousand times that just because she was a stay at home wife and mother didn't mean she didn't work. My parents were about as keen on that statement from her as I was. We wouldn't have thought much about it coming from a stay at home mom and wife that didn't have a child in school, a nanny for when said child wasn't in school and a housekeeper. What she did to fill her time was a constant topic of discussion between me and my parents. At first they tried to keep their opinions to themselves for Chris's sake, but they gave up on that struggle the year Bailey started preschool and nothing had changed.

Yeah, I knew what got at her and I used it. I would have held my tongue if my parents were around, but since they were out shopping at the outlet malls in Destin, Becky was fair game. "So, not pregnant with my second little niece or nephew yet?"

"No! Jesus!" she huffed.

I hit the nerve I intended to. "Sor-ree." I drug out the word for emphasis. "Come on Bailey, the dolphins await."

I picked up Bailey's bag and added it to the items already hung over my arm. Our house was beachfront, but I'd loaded up everything, except the kitchen sink so I wouldn't have to walk back up. The less I had to deal with Becky, the better this week would go.

Down by the water Bailey and I made camp for the day. It was late May and the breeze coming off of the water was brisk that morning. The tent was giving me a fit until two college boys stopped to help me. They hardly waited until the task was over before they started clambering for my information.

"How long are you staying? What's your number? Where's your house?" They stumbled over each other's questions.

They weren't bad looking boys and they seemed nice enough, but I wasn't looking for a beach week fling.

I had trained Bailey well and she came to my rescue right on cue.

"Baby, don't get in the water until I get down there," I yelled to her.

Bailey was all of eight and she looked it. She also looked like a little version of me, honey blonde hair with sun bleached streaks, lightly tanned skinned with a few freckles, same nose, same eyes. She could easily pass for mine. When she turned around and answered, "Yes, Mommy," the color drained from those boys' faces and they couldn't get moving fast enough.

Bailey understood the code. If I called her "Baby" she was to call me "Mommy." If the boys or men, in some cases, didn't get to stepping fast enough, then she was to follow up by asking me when daddy was coming down to play with us. There was only one time when our roleplay didn't work, but Bailey saved me anyway. She pretended to have to go number two and demanded that I take her home. She was quite the little actress. It also helped that I bribed her with ice cream.

Bailey and I played in the surf for a while. We used the binoculars to look for dolphins for another portion of the morning and we had girl talk, which was limited to our favorite shades of nail polish. No less than five members of the opposite sex stopped to chat with me, four of which left appalled that I had a daughter Bailey's age.

"You wanna go for a walk down the beach?" I asked Bailey who was getting bored making sea creatures in the sand.

I was bored, too. I'd gotten the idea that I would read a Jane Austin novel. It was something I'd survived college without doing, but for whatever reason thought now would be a good time to try. It wasn't. It had been an hour and I was only on page ten.

"Yes, let's!" Bailey jumped up and dusted the sand off of her bottom.

While I stood up and put away my book, Bailey grabbed our hats.

"Here," she offered, "You wear mine and I'll wear yours."

"Okay, but we are not trading sunglasses," I told her.

It was one thing to give up my wide-brimmed hat for a fedora, but I was not giving up my Ray-Ban's for some Scooby-Doos.

Bailey and I walked along the edge of the water. Sometimes the waves came in and washed over our feet. Other times it crashed across my shins. Bailey loved running away as if being chased by the waves. Bailey could make a game out of anything. She was lucky to have gotten her imagination from our side of the family.

About ten houses down the beach from ours we came to a tidal pool. The pool was made where the backwaters of Draper Lake flowed toward the Gulf of Mexico. The white sand was eroded as the salt water flowed over the sand bar that separated the two.

Bailey tossed my hat in the sand and went splashing in. She didn't meet a stranger and immediately started chasing hermit crabs with the other children that were playing in the pool. I lingered behind and waded along the edge.

The water in the pool was warm compared to that flowing in the gulf that morning. I was content keeping to myself while Bailey played, but she would have none of that. As far as she was concerned, I was just a big kid there for her entertainment.

"Come on, CC!" You have to help us!" Bailey motioned for me to come out to the middle.

Resistance was futile. Bailey would not take no for an answer. Before I knew it I was the entertainment committee for four little girls and three little boys. The adults that I assumed were with these children sat under their umbrellas, sipping from koozies and acting oblivious to their children.

Hermit crab hunting turned into Marco Polo followed by challenges of who could swim underwater the farthest before coming up for air. I managed to escape the challenge by offering to be the judge.

Around noon the number of children dwindled as the mommies on the shore called their little ones up for lunch. Bailey and one other little boy were all that was left playing in the tidal pool.

"Bailey, are you ready to go get some lunch?" I asked her.

"Not yet. Please, Aunt CC, don't make me go yet."

"Okay."

I had a feeling Bailey would be fine to play all day and decided not to force her to leave. I figured she'd let me know once she got hungry and we could walk back to our tent then.

"Let's play that game where you throw me." Bailey tugged at my arms.

The game only amounted to me picking Bailey up and throwing her toward the deep end of the pool back home. We hadn't done it since last year and I was afraid Bailey might have gotten too big for me to still lift her. She was persistent and I was a pushover.

"I guess." I picked Bailey up and tossed her.

Before Bailey even hit the water the little boy was begging, "Do me! Do me!"

As I contemplated how I was going to turn the little fella down a stern voice came from behind me. "Joshua Belgrave!"

The boy's head whipped around as did mine. The man sounded put out and apparently this was Joshua that was standing next to me.

The man came from the direction of the sun and despite my shades and hat, I was blinded. I could see only the man's figure. He called again for Joshua and the boy waded through the water past me.

"I'm sorry. I hope he wasn't bothering you," the man stepped closer to the water's edge and extended his arms to the child. He was out of breath and frantic sounding and clearly the child's father.

"Oh, he's no bother," I replied as I put up a hand to try to block the sun and get a better look at who was speaking to me.

"Daddy! Daddy! This is Bailey! She's my friend," Joshua exclaimed as he tugged at his father.

"Josh, you scared the life out of me! You cannot just leave the house on your own. Anything could have happened to you!"

"I'm sorry," I apologized about the same time as Josh did. Mine followed with, "I thought he was with the women over there." I gestured to the group of ladies sitting near the sandbar now eating lunch with all of the other children. "If I'd known, we would have brought him home."

"No, it's not your fault," the shadowed figure of the man then gave his own apology.

"Daddy watch me!" Josh demanded. "I can swim all the way across with one breath."

"No, Josh. Come. We should get back home," he insisted, but Josh jerked away and dove under the shallow water.

Bailey immediately dove in behind Josh and the race was on. I focused on the children as they swam half the distance across the tidal pool, about ten yards out from where I was standing. Josh managed to outlast Bailey and popped up after she did.

16

"I guess the swimming lessons paid off," the man commented.

I looked over my shoulder to find him standing almost even with me, but still out of the water. The sun went behind a cloud and what I saw then was the most beautiful man I'd ever laid eyes on. I had turned only to praise Josh's swimming and agree about swimming lessons, but I found myself tongue tied. I stuttered through the words, "He's a... natural."

"Thanks, I'm Jackson," he offered his hand, seemingly oblivious to my reaction to him.

Without my usual cue, Baily sprang into action when she saw him extend his hand and heard the introduction. "Mommy, watch me!"

"Oh, God," I mumbled before calling Bailey to come to me. "Bailey, not now."

If this man was about to hit on me, all bets were off. Unless he was married, and that was a rule I never broke, the anti-summer fling rule could be shattered. The hotness standing next to me was well worth pretending the rule never existed.

"But, Mommy," Bailey protested.

"Bailey, please come here." I asked politely, yet mortified, wondering what he might think.

I knew what he was thinking. He was thinking exactly what I wanted all of the others to think. That same old question was written on his face: how old must I have been when I had her.

"Damn it!" I cursed internally.

Bailey swam over and stood up as I explained, "I'm Caroline and this is Bailey, my niece."

I was about to prod Bailey into confessing, but what would she say? Would she completely out me and our little game? Would she tell him that I made her call me Mommy to get rid of the undesirables?

Chapter 3

"Aunt CC, watch me!" Josh called as he went under and did an hand stand.

Josh saved me. It all happened in a matter of seconds so there was no further delay in my introduction.

"Most everyone calls me CC, except Bailey who calls me Aunt CC. Right, Bailey?" I gave her a wink.

"Yes, ma'am." Bailey grinned and then returned to playing with Josh in the water.

"Josh said he doesn't have any aunts so Bailey told him I could be his aunt, too," I explained as I kept my focus on them.

As it turned out my jig was still up.

"Look, I won't judge you about making her call you mommy to, well...anyway...If you won't judge me for being a crappy father that loses his kid at the beach."

I took my eyes off of the children and I watched him as he spoke. I noticed among other things that he wasn't wearing a wedding band and there was no sign that one that was freshly removed. There was no tan line.

I missed shaking his hand earlier due to Bailey so I offered to shake on it now. "Deal!"

"By the way, everyone calls me Jack," he said as we shook on it.

I smiled and felt faint when he took my hand and smiled back. His smile was like ringing a bell. When he did it, I bet an angel got their wings. My heart fluttered at the sight. It just wasn't natural for a man to be that good looking short of in a magazine or on T.V.

"So, no judgement?" He asked as he released my hand.

I was still tingling from his touch and probably blushing, too. All I could muster in response was to shake my head in the negative.

"How long has Joshua been down here?"

"About an hour."

"Jesus Christ!" He ran his hands through the waves of his dark brown hair. "I'm a shitty father! I'm worse than my father and that's really saying something."

"Don't beat yourself up. He was with Aunt CC." I tried to lighten the mood. "I'm sure you're not that bad."

As soon as the words left my lips I realized how what I said could be interpreted. I meant to assure him he wasn't a bad father, but instead I may have unwillingly insulted his father and agreed that his father was shitty.

I quickly tried to correct any damage. "I mean, I don't have any of my own, but..."

"Of course not, what are you, all of college age?"

I squared my shoulders. "I just graduated college."

"Ah..."

Bailey and her timing. "Aunt CC, you promised the throwing game!" My attention was directed back to the kids as they made their way back toward us.

"Bailey, no. Not right now." I tried to put her off.

"I bet my dad can throw me farther," Josh bragged.

Bailey argued, "I bet he can't."

"Are you up for the challenge, CC?" Jack asked.

"Are you serious?" I looked him over. He wasn't in swim trucks. He was wearing khakis and a white t-shirt with Santa Rosa Beach written across the chest. He wasn't exactly dressed for playing in the water. "You're going to get soaked."

"Bailey, I think your aunt is scared the boys might win." Jack made faces and tickled Bailey.

"Really?" I sized him up again. "I think we have youth on our side. How old are you?" Of course I was only teasing him and luckily he got that.

"I'll have you know, I'm only thirty-two. It's not like I'm forty or have one foot in the grave. Thank you very much!"

"Are you ready, Bailey?" I asked her.

Jack added, "Ladies first," as Bailey answered, "Yes, ma'am."

I picked Bailey up and tossed her with all I had. She was a chunk and as I let go of her, her mother's comments about my bikini echoed in my ears. The vision of my top slipping loose or shifting popped in my mind. I desperately hoped I hadn't just flashed the entire lot of the beach goers. By the time Bailey hit the water I'd already made sure everything was still fully covered.

"Not too high, Daddy," Josh whimpered at the last possible moment.

Jack clearly held back and Josh landed about two feet closer to us than Bailey. From the look of Jack's physique, I was certain he could have launched Josh half the distance of the tidal pool if he'd given it his full effort.

"Girls rule. Boys drool," Bailey taunted Joshua.

"Again, Daddy!" Josh shouted as he raced back to Jack. "This time a little higher."

Of course Bailey was up for another round, too.

"Best two out of three," Jack asked the kids.

"Loser buys lunch," Bailey told him and both mine and his eyes went wide.

"Bailey, honestly. Where do you get these things?" I shrieked.

"Daddy," Bailey was quick with an honest answer.

"Figures," I sighed.

With each throw Joshua got braver and Bailey got heavier. The boys won.

"What's for lunch?" Josh asked me.

"Josh." Jack shook his head.

"Well, we won and the bet was for lunch," Josh stood his ground.

"He's six, not stupid. He knows how a bet works." I gave his father a shrug and a smile. "We have a tent and a fully stocked cooler about ten houses down. Bailey and I are happy to pay up."

"I don't like fish." Josh made a gagging face as he told me.

"You are in luck. We don't have fish," I assured him.

Before Jack could agree Bailey took off running out of the water and down the beach about as fast as her legs would carry her. Joshua chased after her.

"I guess that settles that," I said to Jack as I started out of the pool.

"We really shouldn't impose. I mean, you've already babysat Josh for an hour this morning. I don't want you to have to feed him too."

"It's no trouble. Plus, you're going to have to walk all the way down there to get him now. You might as well have some lunch while there."

It wasn't until we started away from the water that I saw the mothers of the other children that had played with Bailey and Joshua before watching us. I tried not to pay them any attention, but I could tell they were talking about us. I could only hear one of them and I knew I was right. I grabbed my hat out of the sand as I passed them.

"She's all of twenty-two. Of course she looks like that now," the one rolled her eyes and commented to the woman next to her. The two talking were the heaviest set of the group. They were clearly past their prime.

I didn't hear the other one reply, only her next statement. "I know. I guess he just wants a piece of ass. It's been six years since his wife died so maybe..."

I didn't hear what else the women had to say for Jack asking something about peanuts and my mind settling on the notion that his wife was dead.

"Excuse me?" I said.

"Lunch, it's not peanut butter and jelly sandwiches, is it? I don't mean to...It's just that Jack has a peanut allergy."

"Oh, shit!" I took off running. I wasn't sure what Becky or my mother might have packed in the cooler for Bailey.

Bailey and Josh were so far ahead of us they'd surely made it back to our tent. Undoubtedly, Bailey would have offered Josh whatever there was by now. Unlike her mother, she was always so polite. Scantily clad or not, I ran as fast as I could. Jack ran faster and passed me.

"Navy blue, Georgia Tech tent!" I yelled to him in case he really beat me there.

Jack really burned it up running down the beach and beat me to the tent by a good thirty seconds. He was doubled over catching his breath as Josh ate ham and spray cheese on a cracker. The children were oblivious to Jack's second heart attack of the day.

I spread out the beach towels for the kids to picnic on. They ate and discussed the awesomeness of spray cheese.

Jack and I settled into the beach chairs. Luckily, I'd brought down adult chairs in case my parents showed up and left Bailey's kiddie chair at the house.

I pulled out the containers and offered Jack my homemade chicken salad. "No allergies, right?"

"No. This looks great. Thanks." He took the fork and little individual Tupperware container. "Did you make this?"

"I made it and the chocolate chip cookies."

"Did you hear that, Buddy?" Jack leaned down to Josh. "CC made chocolate chip cookies."

Josh jumped up and threw himself around me. "I love having an aunt!" He squeezed so hard I thought my chest was going to be concave when he let go.

I glanced toward Jack and laughed, "If I had only known it was that easy to make boys love me."

He looked me up and down. It was the first time I'd noticed him checking me out. "I can't imagine you have a problem getting boys."

I felt the heat rise in my cheeks and turned my head to keep him from seeing. I moved the bite of chicken salad that I'd just taken to the corner of my mouth. "It's quality not quantity that's the problem."

22

"Touche." Jack replied. I could imagine he had the same problem.

There was a momentary lull in the conversation while we ate. A couple of minutes passed and Jack added, "If you didn't run them off by making them think you have a ten year old..."

"I'm eight!" Bailey promptly corrected him.

"Forgive me," he gave her a wink. "An eight year old."

"She's always listening," I cautioned.

"I know, he hears everything as well," Jack nodded toward Josh as he took another bite of the chicken.

Josh chimed in, "He says I could hear a rat fart in California if I wanted to."

"Joshua Michael Belgrave! No, sir!" Jack said with force as Bailey died laughing.

I leaned over toward Jack and said in a bit lower tone, "Great, now she'll tell her parents she heard the 'f-word' today."

Shortly after lunch Josh asked to use the restroom.

Jack stood. "We really should be going. Thank you so much for lunch and for watching Josh this morning."

"If you want to let them play a little longer, I can run him up to the house to use the restroom there. Our house is right up there."

"Please, Daddy?" Joshua pleaded. "Bailey says we still have to find the dolphins."

"Josh, we really should go. Daddy's got an important call to make this afternoon."

Jack nearly had to resort to threats to get him to leave and I think Bailey and I were as sad as Josh was to see them go. They might have been two years apart, but they played well together. As for me and Jack, he might have been ten years older than me, but I enjoyed his company more than any man in as long as I could remember.

"I hope we see them again," Bailey frowned.

"Me, too." I made the pouty face at her before picking her up and spinning her around.

Chapter 4

Wonders of whether I'd ever see Jack Belgrave and his son again distracted me all evening. Was he just a stranger I met on the beach and was that all he'd ever be? These questions got me through dinner across the table from Becky. Lost in my own thoughts I hardly heard her jabs and criticisms.

Dreams of the finest man I'd ever seen woke me in a sweat. In the dream he kissed me. I woke to the memory of it so vivid that I could still taste him. The dream didn't progress beyond sweet nothings, but I ached for more.

I'd never been attracted to anyone that much older than me before. I'd never given a guy with a kid a second look before either, but I stole every glance at Jack that I could. Seeing him with his son only made him that much more attractive.

Although Becky lived for the beach and relished the status symbol my parents' house provided her, she never ventured too far off of the screened in porch anymore. She'd gotten a nasty case of sun poisoning one year and that kept her pent up on the porch ever since. Because Becky never wanted to sit up there alone, my brother was almost always forced into seclusion with her. It was left to my parents and I to provide Bailey with fun in the sun.

I laid there in my bed thinking of Jack Belgrave and praying to God that I'd see him again. I flopped from side to side unable to go back to sleep, getting excited about the prospect of going back out to the beach when the sun came up. I hoped I would find him and Josh there, too. Josh's parting words to Bailey had been, "See you tomorrow."

The day came and went with no sign of Joshua or his father. Bailey and I played under our tent, in the surf in front of it and we even went down the beach to the tidal pool. If my mother knew about Jack, she'd have sworn I was looking for him and she'd have been right. It went unspoken, but Bailey was looking for Josh as well. She found some of the other children from the day before, but they basically ignored her so we headed back not long after we got there. Both Bailey and I had a twinge of depression over not seeing our new friends, but for all we knew, the Belgrave boys might have packed it up and gone back to their real homes.

Wednesday morning arrived and with it came the news that the sale of the beach house was going through. Depression really was setting in for me. Fearing Bailey was getting too much sun, and probably too close to me, Becky insisted that she stay in the shade and play on the porch.

I couldn't bring myself to set up the tent and sit by the water knowing Bailey couldn't come down. Feeling sorry for Bailey and myself, I couldn't take hanging around at the house all day either so after lunch I went for a walk down the beach in the opposite direction of Draper Lake. I was not myself as I walked along looking out at the gulf thinking this might be one of the last walks I took along the beach. I was sad for my parents, Chris, me, but most of all Bailey. She wouldn't get to grow up here like Chris and I did.

I was about a half mile down the beach when I heard someone calling my name. I wasn't used to being called by my first name so it hardly phased me until he yelled it the second time.

"Caroline, over here!"

I searched the faces along the beach, recognizing the voice. It was Jack. He was standing with an elderly couple and a young woman. The three of them looked wide eyed, but Jack looked genuinely happy to see me as he waved me over.

I was skeptical, but relieved to see him again. My insides jumped with glee, momentarily forgetting my sadness. I walked up the hill where the sand had eroded toward them. As soon as I got within reach, Jack took my hand and pulled me close to his side.

"Caroline, this is Mr. and Mrs. Daniel and their granddaughter, Leslie." Jack gave me a squeeze around my waist. "I've been dying for you to meet them."

Confused, I looked at Jack.

"You know," he returned his gaze to my eyes, "their house is the one right next to my parents' old house and I grew up playing with Leslie."

I started to catch on.

"Oh, right, Leslie, of course. Jack goes on and on."

I wrapped my arm around Jack, but with the other hand I gave his chest a loving pat and looked at him adoringly. It wasn't a stretch. He was dressed for the beach today, no stiff khakis and t-shirt. He was shirtless and in trunks. He was likely going to have to beat the women away with a stick and I didn't mind being that stick.

I quickly turned my attention to Leslie, "You know Jack still can't build a sand castle to save his life." I laughed recalling the attempt he'd made with Josh and Bailey earlier in the week.

"Thank God Caroline loves me for more than my artistic abilities," Jack played along.

My inner monologue kicked in. "Damn straight," I thought to myself. "I love you for your good looks."

"I bet she loves you for a few million reasons," Leslie said under her breath.

I heard exactly what she said, but chose to ignore her. I had to keep in mind I was only acting and this wasn't personal for me. Although a good cat fight would relieve some of my frustrations, I kept in mind that this was Jack's show, his friends and his acquaintances, not mine.

Old Mr. Daniel didn't take his eyes off of me. "We can all see why you love Caroline," he gave Jack a playful punch on the shoulder with his hand that wasn't holding his cane. "You devil, keeping this one all to yourself."

"Granddaddy!" Leslie chided.

Mrs. Daniel chimed in, "You are a beauty, dear, and you look so...young." She sounded so sweet, like butter wouldn't melt in her mouth, but I could tell instantly where Leslie learned her use of tact.

"It was so nice meeting y'all, but we've really got to get back. My parents are waiting on us for lunch. Jack, you know how Mother gets when she doesn't eat on time." I squinched up my nose toward them and shook my head, "Beastly."

I eased away taking his hand with me.

"Right. Right," he agreed.

Each time Jack looked at me it was with doting affection. Inside I was melting. I hated it wasn't real.

Jack continued his goodbyes to the Daniels, "You all will have to join Caroline and me for dinner one night. Caroline is quite the chef."

"We would love to," Mr. Daniel answered for the lot of them while the ladies rolled their eyes.

Knowing they were watching as we walked away, about ten feet away, Jack gave me a slap on my left butt cheek to cement the idea of our relationship in their minds. It caught me completely off guard. It stung and I skipped a step and let out a yelp. I ran and Jack gave chase, catching me and whirling me around off of my feet. When he put me down he took my hand and pulled it to his lips and kissed it. He really was laying it on thick as we continued up the beach hand in hand.

Once out of earshot Jack heaped on the praise. "You were great!"

"You are shameless!" I could not contain the smile on my face.

"We all have our undesirables," Jack laughed. "Now maybe they'll leave me alone about dating Leslie. Thanks for helping me out with that."

"You're welcome, you big fat liar!" I giggled.

"Seriously, the look on their faces when you started walking up was priceless."

"You know you owe me now. Seriously, I need to shower after being mentally groped by Granddaddy." I gave a fake shiver and made a face like I was going to vomit.

"Yeah," Jack cringed too. "Sorry about that and, really, thanks for being a good sport. I really appreciate it."

"You know, I usually buy Bailey ice cream when she helps me out."

"So that's the going rate on renting a girlfriend? A scoop of ice cream?"

"I didn't say I was cheap," I held up my fingers. "Two scoops. Rent on a child is only one scoop."

Jack and I continued laughing and making jokes about our rouse with the Daniels as we walked down the beach. Eventually Jack let go of my hand.

"Sorry about that," he mentioned as he took his hand back.

"Don't worry about it. I would say it will cost you another scoop, but I don't want to sound like an ice cream slut."

Our laughing started all over again. The truth was that I would have bought him the entire ice cream store just to keep holding his hand.

"That's my place up there," Jack pointed to one of the newest beachfront mansions. "Let me run in and grab a shirt, alright?"

Jack's house made ours look like a rat trap. As modern and new as his was, ours was old and outdated. It was two stories with wrap around porches on both levels. It even had a widow's walk on the top and it looked like the perfect spot for watching the stars. I loved our house, but his place made me envious.

Jack's place had French doors in place of windows leading out to the porches. From where I was, it looked like every room let out onto the porch. Hardy plank painted a dark sand-like color with white trim made up the outside. It was amazing. I didn't know much about

29

real estate, but I knew this was in the multimillion dollar range.

The ice cream parlor was up the beach near where his house was so I stopped to wait for Jack outside. Just looking at him from behind as he walked away made me salivate.

"You can come inside if you like," Jack offered when he noticed I hadn't followed.

"Okay."

Jack waited for me to catch up.

"Where's Josh?" I asked him as we headed up the steps.

"The good news is, in case you were wondering, I haven't lost him again."

"Oh, well, um, I didn't mean..."

"I know. It's okay. He's with my parents. My mother likes to take him shopping and to lunch their last day here."

"So y'all are leaving?" I had enough composure to ask it like a normal person, not like a love sick teenager on the verge of heartbreak.

"No, just my parents. Josh and I will be here until school starts back for him."

A wave of relief washed over me. "I'd give anything to be able to stay down here all summer like we used to."

Jack opened the door to into the house and held it for me. "Why can't you stay?"

Jack and I carried the conversation through the porch and into the living room.

"My parents had to sell our house." I couldn't contain the disappointment in my voice then. "I found out this morning that the sale is going through."

"I'm so sorry. I remember you mentioned growing up there in the summers."

I tried to shake it off and not ruin the mood. "I keep telling myself it's just a house, but it feels a bit like losing a member of the family.   I know I'm being ridiculous."

"I know exactly what you mean. I still miss our old house where I grew up. Don't get me wrong, I'm happy to be away from Leslie Daniel, and if you saw it you'd think I was crazy for missing it. But it's where all of my memories are. It's where Josh took his first steps."

"Our house isn't great either and you're right. It's where all of my memories are. I know it's silly, but I always thought I would get married out on the beach right out in front of it and that I'd make memories with my children there."

"Maybe the new owners will put it in the rental pool and you can rent it from time to time." Jack was trying to find a bright spot.

Surveying the living room that bled into the kitchen and dining room, I got the feeling I was in a Coastal Living photo shoot. Our entire house would have fit in half of the downstairs of his house.

"I think the new owners' plan to tear it down and build something like this." I did my best to make that sound like a complement. Since Jack didn't say anything else on the subject, I wasn't sure if I had succeeded.

"Wait here. I'll be right back," Jack then darted up the stairs.

I couldn't help, but to be amazed by this place. It was an interior decorating masterpiece from floor to ceiling. Stark white walls that matched the exact shade of the slip covers on the couch and chairs. The floors were grayish brown wood as far as I could see with a minimal amount of area rugs, which were floral designs with seafoam blue and white. The ceiling matched the wood on the floor, kind of like the bead-board paneling and the rugs matched the throw pillows.

It wasn't overdone in what-nots and trinkets and every seashell collected over the course of thirty years like our house.   It had a ton of candles and they were everywhere.   There were candles in jars with sand and

31

crushed shells in the bottom. There were candles on pillars, candles on sconces on the walls, candles galore, but none appeared to have been lit. The candles just firmed up the idea that everything was just for show including the rock fireplace because who would ever build a fire indoors at the beach?

I was studying the photos on the mantle when Jack returned. There were countless photos of Joshua, some of Jack and Josh together and some with a couple that I imagined were Jack's parents. The resemblance in the two men was uncanny, but Josh looked nothing like either of them. I could only assume he looked like his mother, but there were no pictures of another female anywhere on the mantle.

"You have a lovely family," I remarked, still looking at the photos. "I love this one of Josh."

"Ah, yes, he was two and terrified of Santa." Jack stood next to me admiring it with me.

"But it's priceless. I think my mother has a picture of me just like that."

"Really? All red-faced and veins popping out?"

"Oh, yes, mad as fire and not going to take it anymore. It's at home in Atlanta or I'd offer to show it to you."

Chapter 5

Jack and I left his house and headed up the beach. Feeling under dressed more so than ever with the return of Jack's khakis and t-shirt, I asked if we could stop by my place so I could grab a cover-up.

"Do you mind? You'll probably have to meet my family," I cautioned him.

"That's fine." Jack nudged me. "Come on, let's get going."

"I'll be quick," I promised.

On the porch Bailey immediately noticed who was with me. She'd been playing Go Fish with my father, but popped right up demanding to know where Josh was.

Jack leaned down to Bailey's level. "He's with his grandparents this afternoon. Why don't you introduce me to everyone while Aunt CC gets her cover-up."

The man really had a way with children and all eyes were on him. I heard Bailey making the rounds naming everyone including my father while I ran inside.

I would have sprinted down the hallway toward my room, but my mother was blocking the path. She was packing the linen closet into a box.

"Mama, why don't you wait?" I'll do that when I get back." I offered.

My mother had tears in her eyes as she folded one of the pink beach blankets that we used to lay out for Bailey to take naps on when she was a baby. "It's okay, CC. You go have fun. I'll get this. I want you to enjoy every minute you have left here."

"Mama, seriously," I hugged her and wiped an errant tear away. "Don't cry. We're all okay. It's just a house."

Mama struggled to smile. "I know, but..."

"No, buts. Dry your eyes while I get dressed and come outside with me. There's someone I want you to meet."

33

"I don't know, CC. I'm not fit for company today."

"Mama, I insist. You've got to meet him."

Mama let out a defeated sigh, a noise I was getting used to hearing from her. When I came back her face was freshly washed and a hint of lip gloss had been applied. My mother was a gorgeous woman even at sixty, but she never met people without at least a little makeup on. I was fortunate to take after her is what my father always said. I only hoped I was as pretty as she was.

I took her by the hand and led her to the porch where Jack was waiting on me. My introduction of Jack to my mother was over shadowed by Becky's remarks about my attire.

"Shorts and a tank top." She let out a huff in the middle of her sentence. "That's the most she's had on all week."

It was all I could do not to lose it and tell her how much I hated her once and for all. My face turned red and I gritted my teeth through telling my mother, "This is Jack Belgrave. Bailey and I met him and his son on the beach Monday."

Mama shot a look at Daddy and he gave her a nod. Words weren't exchanged, but they had a silent conversation between themselves.

"It's nice to meet you, Mr. Belgrave." I was puzzled by my mother's formality.

"Please, call me Jack."

"I'm Carol and it's nice to meet you. Could I get you a glass of tea or something?" My mother was the picture of Southern hospitality.

"No, ma'am. Thank you anyway. CC and I were just going to walk up the street for ice cream," Jack declined.

With Bailey hanging on his every word she immediately began asking to come with us. Before Jack or I could answer, Becky told her to get her cover-up and flip-flops. I could have died. I looked to my brother for help, but he was nose deep in the latest Dean Koontz novel and

34

hadn't heard a thing. Neither he nor Becky offered a dime to Jack to cover Bailey, but my father stepped forward to give Bailey five dollars when she ran back out raring to go.

Jack was so sweet about it. As I made a mental note to have a word with my brother later, Jack insisted he would take care of Bailey and stopped my father just shy of passing the bill to her. I just glared at my brother and his sorry wife.

Ice cream with Jack and Bailey definitely cheered me up. I thought maybe Jack would make a move. We were having so much fun and hitting it off. All of the signs were there that he liked me. He didn't make a move. Other than sitting really close to me on the bench outside of the ice cream parlor while we ate, he did nothing. He didn't even reach for my hand on the walk home. He even let Bailey get between us to hold our hands. She was the link between us. I got the feeling he was purposefully avoiding making a move.

Back at the house, Bailey bopped up the steps to brag to Pops, that's what she called my dad, that the chocolate was the best she'd ever had. "It had frozen strawberry chunks!"

I made Bailey thank Jack before she headed up and now I thanked him. "Thanks for everything today. If you need to rent a girlfriend again, I'm your girl." He still didn't make a move so I concluded with, "See you around."

I turned to head up the steps to our porch, but he stopped me. "Hey, CC?"

I stopped on the top step and looked back to find him at the bottom.

"Are you and Bailey going to be putting out that tent of yours tomorrow?"

I gave him a puzzled look. "Probably."

"Good because the wind shredded our tent. All Josh has talked about for two days is his new friends Bailey and Aunt CC. Neither of us have made new friends in so long I can't remember."

The color drained from my face. "Double shit!" I thought. "I've been relegated to the friend category." I wondered if he was about to slug me on the arm or high-five me.

"We'll drink to new friends tomorrow. Bailey and I will be out around 10:00 a.m.," I said out loud.

The rest of the night I flew under the radar around the house.

Thursday and Friday Jack and Josh joined Bailey and I under our tent. My parents packed the house and my brother and sister-in-law stayed laid-up on the porch. I was constantly torn between hanging out with Jack and the kids on the beach and helping my parents.

"Babysitting Bailey and keeping her distracted is enough," my mother assured me.

Bailey introduced Josh to her dolls and he introduced her to Hot Wheels cars and monster trucks. The cars and monster trucks went over way better than the dolls. They spent hours burying them in the sand, building roads for them and ramps to launch them.

Jack brought a cooler each day to share with Bailey and me, the same as we had shared with them. On Thursday, he introduced me to Grolsh beer. I wasn't much of a drinker, but the green bottle and hinge top let me know it was expensive. My father liked it when he wandered down to the beach and sat with us for a while.

On Friday I was introduced to pecan crusted chocolate strawberries by way of Jack feeding one to me.

"My mother's trying a new recipe," he described before instructing me to open my mouth.

Forgetting my manners, I gushed over them while chewing. "These are awesome!"

The chocolate was silky and the perfect contrast to the crunch of the pecans and the tartness of the strawberries. I could have eaten the entire container, but limited myself to only two and the second one I put in my mouth by my own accord.

A little after 2:00 p.m. on Friday I spotted Leslie Daniel strolling up the beach toward us. Her grandparents were close behind. The children were jumping waves at the edge of the shore and Jack was with them. Leslie was bound to see them.

Fearing Bailey would out us, I called her up from the water and sent her to the house to have her mother reapply her sunscreen. Once Bailey was on her way, I left my beach chair and joined the boys in the water. When Bailey got out, Josh pulled his snorkel mask down and began thrashing about trying to find sand dollars. Jack stood there watching and had no idea anyone was near him when I slipped my arm around his waist.

Jack flinched and I whispered, "Here come the Daniels and you are going to owe me some ice cream."

I tilted my head and nodded backward giving Jack the indication of where they were. He glanced over my head and by the look on his face I knew he'd spotted them, too.

"Ready to give them something to talk about?" Jack gave me a once over and pulled me close. The tone of his voice and the way he locked eyes with me, it was sultry and my knees went weak.

The two letter response hitched in my throat, "O...k."

Jack's hand went from my hip to the small of my back and my breath caught as he pulled me closer, so close that I could feel the hair from his happy trail leave tickles across my belly. His other hand grazed past my cheek and went into my hair, which he took by the fistful and pulled my head back. His eyes never unlocked from mine and I was melting. For a moment there was no one else on the beach and then he kissed me and there was no one else on the planet.

Deep and sensual, Jack explored my mouth with his tongue. Holy, God, it was unlike anything I'd ever experienced in my twenty-two years.

37

The waves crashed against my legs and I stood on my toes to reach Jack better. Chill bumps sprang up and down my legs, but not from the temperature of the water. My chest swelled as I pressed into him. The kiss was damn near orgasmic and I did my best to give back all that I got.

When it started my arms were draped loosely over his shoulders and around his neck, but by the time he eased back, I was hanging on tight with my fingers in his hair. There wasn't an inch of me that wasn't turned on by Jack.

"Wow!' Jack licked his lips. "I will definitely write a glowing recommendation to the Rent a Girlfriend Agency on your behalf."

I batted my eyelids, still flustered, and repeatedly reminded myself that it was just a game. No matter how many times I said it in my head, it didn't feel like a game. That kiss felt like way more, way too real.

"Aunt CC," Bailey called as she ran toward us.

Regaining my senses I stepped back from Jack. The Daniels had turned around and headed back down the beach. Joshua was still bobbing with the waves and his snorkeling gear.

Bailey got closer and yelled to me again. "Mama said its time for you to come in."

My head snapped back. "Excuse me?" I said as I emerged from the water and met Bailey at the tent.

Becky had undoubtedly seen the kiss. She never missed a thing or an opportunity to try to ruin things. It infuriated me and my heart rate, which was just starting to settle, quickened again, but not in a good way.

I didn't scream my response over the beach and up to the porch to Becky. Instead, I kept my composure and asked Jack if he and Josh would like to take a walk up the beach.

Jack agreed and while he pulled Josh from the water, I dealt with my sister-in-law. I bent down and placed a peck on Bailey's forehead. "Please go back up and explain to your mother that I said I am an adult and I will come in when I am good and ready. Please say it respectfully so that you will not get in trouble. Thank you, sweetie."

I hated to do it to Bailey, but I knew my reply would gall Becky. Plus, when Bailey noticed we were gone and she was going to have to stay at the house, she'd pester the living fire out of Becky until we came back. I would miss Bailey, but if my brother took his family and left for home right then, I could have my final days at the beach house in peace with my parents and Jack and Josh.

Bailey bounced away, up to the house, and I turned my focus back to Josh and Jack. I grabbed my hat and joined them as they headed toward the tidal pool.

"Hey, Josh, wanna play a game?" I asked him.

"Okay, Aunt CC!" When Josh wasn't hanging on Bailey's every word, he hung on mine. He was a sweet boy with blue eyes like his father and the most adorable dimples when he smiled.

"Whoever finds the biggest seashell on our walk wins." I explained. "It's that easy. I bet I'll find a bigger one than you."

Josh immediately started scanning the ground out ahead of us. "No you won't!" Josh took off ahead of us.

"I know I'm just the paid help, the rented girlfriend and all, but what's the real deal with you and Leslie Daniel?" I asked Jack as we navigated the sand, following along behind Josh.

Jack chuckled. "What makes you ask?"

"Because, that back there, well, I'm not sure if you were trying to help her move on or make her jealous."

Jack laughed again, "Seriously, CC, we went on one date. It was right after my wife died. It was awful. I mean, awful," he emphasized.

"That bad?"

"I was in no mood for dating, but my mother insisted I needed to get out with someone other than an infant or my parents, someone my own age. Thinking it would be harmless, my mother suggested Leslie and I went along so Mother would leave me alone."

I had a misstep and Jack caught me. "Sorry."

"Are you okay?" He said as he righted me.

"Yeah, just clumsy. Go on."

"I could hardly focus on making conversation with her, but I really didn't need to. She made enough for the both of us. Nonstop. I thought my ears were going to bleed. That nasally voice of hers. It was, for lack of a better word..."

"Awful?" I smiled with sympathy.

"She was the definition of trying too hard. And, I have very specific tastes."

The words, "specific tastes," stuck in my head. "Oh, shit!" I thought, "He's gay." My color started to drain.

Without stopping myself, I mumbled, "That explains it."

"Explains what?" He wasn't supposed to hear that, but he did.

"Nothing."

"Come on now. If you have something to say..."

I stopped and watched Josh continue ahead of us a little ways.

Jack stopped and stood there. "What?"

"You're gay."

"What?!!!"

"Specific tastes," I repeated back to him.

"Jesus, CC!" He spun to face me, blocking my view of Josh.

"But..."

Jack closed the gap between us. He locked eyes with me much the same as he had done before the kiss. The heat in me was already on the rise in the few short seconds before he spoke again. I could hardly look up at him. He towered over me by about five inches.

40

"Let me assure you, Caroline, if I was even five years younger, I would ravage you. You would not stand a chance."

I was speechless.

Chapter 6

No boy had ever talked to me like that. No boy had ever made me wet with one word before either. I wasn't dealing with a boy and I think that was the point Jack was making. I was dealing with a man.

My jaw was on the ground and my mouth draped open. I stumbled two steps. What was I supposed to do with that information?

This was like the time Chris and I found where Mama hid the Christmas presents. We knew what our big present was, but we couldn't have it until Christmas. Jack was the Christmas present I couldn't have for the indefinite future. He was the toy I'd been begging for, right there in front of me, but I couldn't play with him. Looking at him was torture. Being that close to him, torture.

I was still spinning when Josh came running up. He tugged at my hand.

"Aunt CC, look what I found!" Josh jumped about, proud of himself having found a sand dollar the size of the palm of, not my hand, but Jack's, which was one and a half times the size of mine.

I quickly sprang into action, praising him. "I think you've just won our game! I don't know how I can compete with that."

"I won! I won!" Josh exclaimed.

"That's awesome, son!" Jack joined in.

"Let's go back to the house and show Bailey and I'll find a prize for you," I told Josh.

This was just the excuse I needed to get away from Jack. My poor heart could not take much more of him right then. The fun in the game we had been playing had come to an end for me. With all of the drama going on with losing our house and now my spirits crushed over Jack, I just wanted to go home, home to Atlanta.

Back at my parents' house I found a prize for Josh. Since Mom was cleaning out the house of our personal effects and Chris hadn't taken the thing home with him years ago, I figured I'd give Josh the five gallon bucket containing all of Chris's old Hot Wheels and Matchbox cars.

Jack and Josh waited on the porch with Bailey, Becky and Chris while I went in to get the bucket.

"Here," I said as I sat the bucket down in front of Josh.

"I haven't seen that thing in years," Chris commented as he swung his feet around and sat up right on the side of the lounge chair.

I picked one of the cars from the bucket and showed it to Josh. "If you turn them over, it will tell you the make and model of the car." I flipped it over and held it up for him to see as I pointed to the writing. "1962 Chevrolet Corvette Stingray."

Chris picked a car too and read the bottom of it. "1973 Mustang II."

"Quite possibly the ugliest car ever built," Jack observed over Chris's selection.

"That is soooo cool!" Josh's eyes almost went cross studying the bottom of the car.

"What do you think you're doing?" Becky asked me as I slid the bucket in front of Josh.

I didn't respond to her and she repeated herself and added, "You can't give those away!"

Completely beyond tired of ignoring her and having her not take the hint, I replied, "Since you cannot seem to take the hint, I am going to tell you once and for all, I am a grown adult and I do not need nor do I want your permission to do anything. Please do not make me embarrass us further by making me repeat myself."

Becky gasped! She stood from her spot next to Chris and stormed inside. Chris followed after her. Bailey continued her game of checkers with my dad and neither of them budged.

"Maybe you and your dad could go home and play with these." I handed Jack the bucket and ushered Josh to the door. Jack followed. "I'm so sorry y'all had to see that."

"It's okay." Jack caught the handle of the screened door and held it for me and Josh. "I'll take the tent down for you so you won't have to deal with that. I've got a feeling you've got a lot to deal with."

"Yeah and it's high time I dealt with it, too, but you don't have to get the tent. I'll get it later."

"Are you sure? Josh and I can have it down in a jiffy."

"No, I still have to get our cooler and everything."

"Well, good luck with everything and I hope we'll see you and Bailey tomorrow. Josh, go get our things from the tent while I say goodbye to CC."

"Yes, sir," Josh replied and then scurried away.

I watched Josh as he went. I was still having a hard time looking at Jack. "I'm not sure about tomorrow," I shrugged. "I might grab my things and head back to Atlanta tonight."

"Promise me you won't do that." Jack was adamant.

I was a bit put off by his tone. "I can't promise you anything."

"I won't have you driving seven hours in the dark by yourself."

"What's it to you? Our ages might not be five years apart, but I am a big girl. I've been taking care of myself well before I met you."

"Are you mad with me?" The look on his face fell at the thought.

"No, but there's nothing but drama for me here and it's not how I want to remember this place." I shook my head, begging him to understand.

"We're friends right?" Jack asked.

"Sure." I gave a slight smile. I'd cast aside my rule about a beach fling only to end up friends with him. I wanted more, but oh well.

"Then, I'm asking you as a friend, please wait until tomorrow morning before getting on the road. It's just not safe."

"Fine."

"Don't lie to me, Caroline!"

I liked when he called me by my name. Hardly anyone else ever did that.

"I'm not lying."

"Good because if I find out you are," he paused, clearly thinking of how he could threaten me. "Because I'll call the agency and all of your hard work will be undone. You'll get a reprimand." Jack shrugged his shoulders as he referred to the game. "You don't want that?"

"Of course not," I rolled my eyes and shook my head.

"I mean, I might need your services in the future and..."

I cut him off. "I get the picture."

"I'm just saying, you wouldn't want me to have to get another girl."

"I'd like to see you try. There's no one that knows your specific tastes the way I do."

Jack cocked an eyebrow at me and flashed that million dollar smile of his. "Exactly."

"Well, you better get going. Josh is waiting."

"Maybe I'll see you tomorrow."

"Maybe."

The word "maybe" seemed a little like goodbye and my heart broke as I watched them walk down the beach. About a fifty yards down, Jack and Josh turned and waved at me. I reciprocated and then went inside.

I opened the door to find the place packed almost down to the bare bones. We weren't supposed to head out until Sunday, but Mama had the whole place cleaned out except for the furnishings. She was taking glasses from the kitchen cabinets and wrapping them for putting them in the boxes. I went around the kitchen island and started helping her.

"Let's get Daddy and go to dinner, just the three of us," I said to her as I started with the cabinet that held the stoneware plates.

Mama loved Bud and Alley's in Seaside so I suggested we go there.

"You never know when we might get back down here," I added with a frown.

"What about your beau? You don't want to go out to dinner with him at least once?" she asked.

I straightened up. "He's not my beau."

"Could have fooled me." She gave me that look she gives us when she catches either Chris or I lying.

"He's not," I replied and I'm sure she could hear the defeat in my voice.

"I may not have gotten out much this week, but I was out and witnessed that kiss on the beach earlier," Mama pointed out.

"I think everyone witnessed it." I turned up my nose.

"Yeah." Mama's opinion of Becky was the same as mine. For a long time she tried to stay neutral for Chris's sake.

"Where is the witch anyway?" I looked around to make sure Becky wasn't lurking somewhere.

"They're out front. Chris is washing the car and she's probably supervising." Mama's neutrality was slipping.

"Let's get out of here and go to dinner, Mama. Like I told Jack, I don't want my last memories of this place to be all about her. All of my best childhood memories revolve around this place and I don't want her to steal them with her nastiness. Please, Mama," I begged.

"Okay, CC, but please don't say anything to your father about losing your memories. He feels bad enough about all of this." My mother had tears in her eyes and I couldn't refuse her. I immediately wished I hadn't put things like that.

"Mama, I know not to say anything to Daddy. I know none of this is his fault."

"Go get changed and then I'll get him to wrap it up with Bailey."

"Yes, ma'am."

I was changed and ready to go within fifteen minutes. I showered and threw on jean shorts, local logo t-shirt and flip flops and a little bit of makeup. I towel dried my hair and pulled it up in a bun. It would have to dry on its own. I mainly wanted to get on the road with Mama and Daddy before Chris and Becky had the chance to catch on and insist on coming with us. I couldn't remember the last time I'd been allowed any alone time with my own parents. Even on the weekends that I came home from college Becky found out and made sure they came down for the weekend too. It had gotten so ridiculous that I only saw my parents alone if I pressured them into coming up to Athens.

"Bill, grab your wallet and come on," Mama stuck her head out onto the porch and told Daddy. "We're going to dinner with CC tonight."

"Mama, I'll treat. Just tell him to come on," I added.

Mama turned and looked at me, "You don't have to pay, CC."

"I don't mind. I invited y'all so I'll pay." I didn't mind paying. They'd paid for my entire college and this entire vacation. One meal in return was the least I could do.

"Bailey," Daddy said, "we'll pick this game up again when I get back. Why don't you come inside and play with your dolls for a little while."

"Can I come to dinner, too?" Bailey asked my parents.

My mother quickly took over the conversation with Bailey. "Not this time, honey, Granddaddy and I are

47

going to have some alone time with Aunt CC like you've had with her the last few days. Okay?"

"Okay," Bailey gave a slight frown, but didn't protest further.

From where I was standing in the living room, I could see through the window, through the porch and out to the beach. Our tent had been taken down and all of our belongings stacked by the door to the porch. When Daddy came in I thanked him for getting everything up.

Bailey came in right behind Daddy and before he could correct my assumption, she did. "Granddaddy didn't do that. Granddaddy went to the bathroom and when he came back Mr. Jack and Josh were almost finished. They asked me where to put everything when they brought it up and I told them we usually left it by the door to use tomorrow."

My face flushed as my mother cut her eyes at me. "No your beau, huh?"

I didn't respond. Instead, I told Bailey I would bring her back a dessert since she wasn't getting to go this time.

"Something chocolate?" Bailey's face lit up.

"Of course." I hugged her and gave her a kiss.

Daddy grabbed his wallet. Mama got her purse. I got my car keys and everything else I needed was already in my pockets. One by one we filed through the door to the driveway.

"Where are y'all going?" Becky did her best to sound sweet about her inquisition. It didn't come off sweet to any of us.

"If you must know, CC is taking us out to dinner." Daddy answered her as Mama and I continued to my car.

"Well, give us a minute and we'll be ready to go," Becky replied, cutting off the water hose and motioning for Chris.

"I'm sorry. I think you misunderstood. CC's taking us out tonight. Maybe you and Chris can take us out tomorrow night." Daddy made the offer for Chris and

Becky to take them out knowing as well as I did that she'd never let that happen. Spending money was a one way street and that street only ran in Becky and Chris's direction.

Becky gave me a glaring look and I waved to her from behind the wheel of my car as Daddy got in.

I backed the car out and mumbled, "One of these days I'm not just going to kill her with kindness."

"Watch it, CC. Your claws are showing." Mama looked at me firmly through the rearview window.

"Carol, I think it's time we stayed out of it," Daddy turned around to Mama.

"What do you mean?" she asked him, obviously shocked that he would say such a thing.

"Would you continually ask CC to turn the other cheek if this was anyone else that was constantly at her?"

"Well..." Mama stuttered and stammered. "But..."

"Exactly. It's been ten years. I'd say Becky's made herself fair game and since Chris hasn't put her on a leash, it might be high time CC gave her what's she's got coming. Don't you?"

"I love you, Daddy." I patted him on the leg.

"I'm not saying pick a fight, CC, I'm just saying if she starts it, then I'm fine with you finishing it once and for all."

"What about Chris?" Mama asked.

"It's about time he stood up to her, too, but that's between him and her," Daddy told her.

I glanced in the rearview mirror at Mama again and she had one of those, "What can I say?" looks on her face.

Chapter 7

After everything was said and done that night, I found myself walking on the beach alone. It was dark on the beach. All porch lights were out on account of not drawing the sea turtles hatchlings in the wrong direction. I didn't know where I was going until I saw the outline of the mansion, a beacon among all of the one story ranch style beach cottages.

I picked up my pace and ran as best as I could through the soft, shifting sand. I feared Josh would be in bed and didn't want to wake him so I knocked lightly. More disturbing was likely the sound of my sniffling back the tears over the sound of the tapping on the door.

I was just about to give up when Jack came to the door.

One look at me and he knew, but asked anyway, "Caroline?"

I wiped under one eye and then the other, dragging the tears off of my cheeks. I tried to smile and make light of my condition. "I need to rent a boyfriend for a little while."

"Of course." Jack held the door, inviting me in.

I fell into his arms just inside the doorway. "I'm sorry, I'm not pretty when I cry," I apologized as the tears started coming again.

"Oh, stop that," Jack stroked my hair from the crown of my head down my back, "You're the most beautiful girl no matter what."

I pulled back, almost repulsed. "I'm sorry. This was a bad idea." I sniffled a time or two. "I can't play this game with you right now."

Jack didn't let go and pulled me back to him. He wrapped his arms around me and I could feel his strength. "No games. You are so beautiful that even I'm intimidated by you."

"That's funny." I sniffled again and hung on to him. "A senator's intimidated by me."

"You finally found out," he sighed.

"My parents told me at dinner. My father said you're the youngest in Florida history." I gathered my breath and asked, "Why didn't you tell me?"

"It's something most everyone already knows. Plus, how did it ever come up in conversation? It's not like I would just announce..."

"That you're basically Florida royalty?" My tears were dissipating. Just talking to him helped. Just talking about something other than my spiteful sister-in-law helped.

"I wouldn't go that far. Anyway, it was nice being anonymous for a change, just being a regular guy. I didn't have to watch what I said to you or worry if you were only interested in me... I mean..."

"It's okay. I understand."

Slipping his hands over mine, Jack put a little space between us. Those blue eyes of his, only lit by the dimmest of porch lights, beamed over me.

"You wanna sit down?" he asked. "Can I get you something to drink?"

"I hate to impose."

"I'm going to get a beer. What would you like? Coke, sprite, a glass of wine? I know you didn't really like the beer the other day."

"Chardonnay, if you have it? Thanks!" I hated letting him go even for the minute or two it would take him to get the drinks and come back.

While Jack was gone, I took a seat on one of the lounge chairs. The cushion on it was as soft as any bed I'd ever slept in. I assessed the furnishings on the porch and came to the conclusion that no expense had been spared. I thought about Becky, how she'd come from nothing and what just making it to the status of our family made her. I couldn't help but wonder what marrying into a family like this would have done to her character. With us she was

51

just nasty and entitled acting, but with this type of wealth she might have really lost her mind and started slithering the streets spitting venom.

I wiped my face one more time before Jack emerged from the house, balancing the beer and wine glass in one hand, a washcloth and two ibuprofen in his other hand.

"Here, take this." He offered the washcloth first.

I took the washcloth and wiped my face. "Thanks!"

"Now these."

He traded me the washcloth for the ibuprofen and the wine. Jack tossed the washcloth on the table next to the lounge chair.

"Scoot up," he instructed me as I washed down the ibuprofen with the wine.

I did as I was asked and Jack slung a leg over and slipped in behind me and the back of the chair. Once in place, he put his arms around me and pulled me back against him. I'd never noticed cologne or after shave on him before, but tonight he had a smell of cedar infused with clean linen, like a very manly dryer sheet.

"You wanna tell me what happened?" He laid my head next to his face and I could feel the trace of stubble on my temple and his breath slip over my cheek.

"As my rented boyfriend or my friend?" I replied with lower volume.

"Whatever you need me to be."

I let out a huff and slightly shook my head. What I needed, and wanted, didn't have the word "rented" anywhere near it.

"I took my parents to dinner tonight and we had a blast. I drove them over to my mother's favorite restaurant in Seaside, my treat. It's been a rough time for them, but for a while we were able to forget and things were normal. Then, we went back to the house."

I carried on and Jack just listened. I'd never felt safe to talk to any of the boys I'd dated in the past the way I felt talking to him. I never felt they really listened, but there was something about him that just made me know that he did listen and that he cared. I don't know why he cared, but I believed he did.

"When we got back to the house, the tension was the kind you could cut with a knife. Chris was packing their room and Becky was sitting on the couch with her feet up. I found Bailey in my room and she was in tears. I asked her what was wrong and she said, 'I hate Granddaddy!' I encouraged her to elaborate on why she would say such an awful thing. She told me that her mother told her that Granddaddy had been a fool with his money and we weren't ever going to be able to come to the beach again because of him."

Jack's chest tensed behind me.

"You can imagine how this infuriated me."

"You see, my sister-in-law isn't much better than poor white trash. She met my brother in college. She was studying to be a nurse and she saved him from one of his diabetic episodes one day. Chris is a diabetic. He has been since childhood, but half the time he forgets to take his insulin. Even to this day, we all worry about him."

"Anyway, he was over the moon for her and, my parents were star struck, too. A nurse, that was perfect for Chris. They wouldn't have to worry about him so much anymore."

"Well, my parents were wealthy, but we never really knew it. Chris and I were pretty sheltered. Our mother worked. Our father worked. Our parents had a really average house in a nice area of town, but we took for granted that everyone had those things because everyone we knew did. We were also taught that it was their house. Taught that they had worked hard for it, not us. It wasn't our house. Then Becky came along. I think she had dollar signs in her eyes from the moment she saw the house. Apparently she was never given the speech about it being her parents' house that she grew up in because to her, especially after she and Chris married, everything that

53

belonged to our parents' belonged to Chris and through him it belonged to her."

"From the moment we met, I was the competition. I stood in the way of what was hers. That's how she treated me. I think her sole purpose in coming around the family was to try to stake her claim and run me off. The thing was, I never saw her as competition. I always tried to be nice to her. The more I tried, the more she took advantage. I tried harder after Bailey came along so I became a convenient babysitter, but also I stood in the way of her child getting what was rightfully hers. I've tried and tried and tried not to say anything for Chris and Bailey's sake. Plus, my parents always begged me to just let it roll off. They were trying to keep the peace for Chris and Bailey as well."

"You know," I turned around and looked at Jack, "my father told me on the way over that he didn't expect me to turn the other cheek anymore. So, when we got back and Bailey repeated what her mother told her about my father, and after knowing how my parents have subsidized them for years, it just flew all over me. My father also told me not to pick a fight, but I was welcome to finish it if she started one."

"What did you do?" Jack asked.

"I ignored my father and picked a fight. I know I shouldn't have. I should've just gone back to Atlanta, but..."

"You'd promised me?" Jack raised the question a bit sheepishly.

"Yes, I promised you."

"So what happened?"

"I made sure my father was in the shower where he couldn't hear me. I gave Bailey the dessert I'd brought her back from Bud and Alley's and sent her to the porch to eat it with my mother. As soon as I closed the door behind Bailey, I turned to Becky and asked her, 'What do you mean telling Bailey the reason she can't come to the beach anymore is because of my father?'"

54

"'Well, it is! If he hadn't been so foolish with his money none of us would be in this spot!' Becky snapped at me."

"What spot exactly is it that you are in? From where I stand it's my parents that are in a spot. You can get off your fat ass and get a job any time now."

"Of course she shot back at me, 'You're just jealous because...'"

"I cut her off, 'Oh do elaborate on that one. Please explain to me what it is about you that I would be jealous about? I mean, you continually try to tell me what to wear, when to talk and what to say. If you think I'm jealous of you because you're somehow smarter than me, rest assured that's not true. I made damn near a perfect score on the GMAT and the LSAT. So what else is there? I'm not jealous of your body, though you constantly try to tell me to cover mine up. And, I am confident enough in my own abilities that I don't have to fetch a man to support me or bribe his parents with their grandchild to get me where I want to be in life. I don't have to bully or act nasty or hateful. So please, enlighten me as to why on Earth you would ever think I would be jealous of you?'"

I probably told Jack too much about myself in repeating my rant, but there it was, out in the open. That didn't stop me from continuing the story.

"'You are a bitch that throws herself at every man that passes!' she screamed at me. 'She accused me of having everything in life handed to me and not having worked a day in my life.'"

"I popped back at her and basically called her a whore. That the only reason she got anywhere at all in life was because she was the only woman that ever gave him head."

Jack commented, "Ouch."

"Yeah, not my finest moment," I admitted.

I continued, "Becky wasn't to be outdone and apparently I really hit a nerve with that one and she slapped me. My father just so happened to be out of the shower and witnessed the slap."

"What did he do?" Jack was sucked in like an old lady watching a soap opera.

"He screamed for Chris to get in there. Chris came running and my father told him to get his bitch on a leash and get her out of his house. He also gave Becky a good what for about how dare she ever raise a hand to either of his children. Becky tried to explain and my father asked her was it the 'get' or the 'out' that confused her."

"If my face wasn't hurting so bad from the sting of her slap I probably would have laughed. I also didn't laugh because Becky yelled for Bailey to get inside and pack her things."

"Jack, I feel absolutely terrible," I started to cry again. "I may have cost all of us a relationship with Bailey."

"Oh no, Caroline, this isn't your fault. Even when Josh and I were around we could see how your sister-in-law was. She was awful to you at every opportunity and who hands off their kid to someone that they can't stand? All she was about was dragging you down. Don't you know that's half the reason she always stuck you with Bailey? It's not like you ever told her that you used Bailey to keep men from bothering you. She stuck you with Bailey as a way to make you as miserable as she was, but what she fails to realize about you is that you loved being with Bailey and that you make everything fun. You have the Midas Touch and she hates you for it."

"The Midas Touch? Really?"

"You know what I mean. You make everything better when you're around and people like your sister-in-law hate people like you. There's nothing you could've done to have made her like you and you certainly aren't the one that's destroyed any relationships for Bailey. One day Bailey will see and she'll thank her mother for that."

"What about my parents? They are going to hate me. I caused them to lose Bailey?" I sobbed.

Jack pulled me close to him. "You can cry it out all you want, but you didn't cause anything."

I'm not sure how long Jack and I sat there, his arms around me and my head leaned back on his chest. Just feeling the rhythm of his breathing, the rise and fall of his chest, was comforting. He was older and wiser and I trusted him implicitly. I hoped he was right that I hadn't cost my parents their relationship with Bailey and, if I had, I hoped it hadn't cost me my relationship with them.

The night was so peaceful. There was just the crashing of the waves with the tide to provide a soundtrack to the night. Jack finally broke the silence and urged me up. "Come with me. I want to show you something."

I raised up and Jack stood. He offered his hand to help me up, but he didn't take it back once I was on my feet. He kept hold and led me into the house. We went up the stairs to the second floor, but he didn't stop. We went up again, to the crow's nest.

"I told you I miss our old house. This makes me miss it a little less."

Jack hit a switch and the entire roof retracted and the night sky opened above me.

"Just when I thought you couldn't get any cooler, you go and do something like that." I wrapped an arm around Jack's waist and gave him a sidearm hug as I looked around in wonder.

It wasn't like it was needed, but there was a telescope in the middle of the room.

"If my mother hadn't warned me that it was a bad idea for me to sleep way up here while Josh is downstairs, I would have drug a bed up here. She made me put this thing up instead." Jack motioned toward the telescope.

"I would just make him sleep up here with me. It would be like camping out."

Jack did that thing he did, when he was amused. It was like a guarded laugh. "I bet you would.

"I would!"

57

Jack turned our focus back to the stars. "There's nothing like looking at the stars to make all of your problems seem small. That's what I always think when I come up here."

"I guess when put like that."

Jack stood there admiring the sky and I stood there admiring him. I pressed my luck and faced him. "Could my rented boyfriend indulge me one more thing tonight?"

Jack readily agreed without knowing my request.

I took his face in my hands and tilted him toward me. I went to my toes and stretched up so I could reach him. I pressed myself to him and paused for a moment, just taking every line on his face in, every whisker that went untrimmed.

The pause, the time I spent memorizing his face, made him come to me. One hand secured me to him by my hip and the other around the back of my neck. He gifted me with a kiss, the twin of the one from earlier in the afternoon. That's exactly what I wanted.

Jack was a master at the use of his tongue. He was so good that this time my mind was completely void of any other thoughts but his voice in my head, "I would ravage you."

Was this the beginning of that? Had Jack lost himself to the moment as I had? Had he put away the foolishness about being five years younger?

The influence of his body pressing harder to mine sent me stumbling, quick stepped, backward until I felt the wall at my back. There was a thud, but he didn't break the seal between us. He took my hands in his and raised them above my head. Everything about me readied for sex. My breasts swelled as well as other regions of my body.

Down my arms his hands slid, the perfect contraction of light as a feather and firm, down he went back to my hips and pulled me closer to him. I hooked my leg around his and balanced on one foot, both of us pulling at the other ever closer. I could feel him through the khaki shorts. A tickle rose between my legs and in this moment I knew without doubt he could do what he said he would.

One week of knowing Jack and I wanted him like I'd never wanted anyone. The very few boys I'd been with I made wait and wait and wait. I made them work for me. Compared to the way I was with them, I'd have given myself to Jack on a whim. Perhaps it was my turn to work.

Realizing his hands were at the button of my shorts, Jack came to his senses and promptly pulled back. "Forgive me."

"What's to forgive?" I stammered.

I longed to have the stubble of his face scratching over mine again. Instead he leaned into me, burying his face in my hair. I clung to him and wished with all my might that he was mine.

Chapter 8

Jack insisted on walking me back home even though I assured him it wasn't necessary.

"Honestly, Josh sleeps like the dead. It will be fifteen minutes and he'll never even know I was gone."

"I don't want to put you out."

As much as I never wanted to leave him, I had to get home and getting home meant getting myself back in order. I could not explain it to Jack, but I needed the time away from him to regain my composure before facing my parents. The blood drawn to the surface of my skin where he'd kissed me and where his whiskers had rubbed me to a chafed condition needed to subside.

I left my parents' house all red faced and in tears and I hesitated returning equally red, but for drastically different reasons. I still feared I'd tarnished the relationships between my parents and my brother and his family, especially their relationship with Bailey. I didn't dare face them in my current state.

Jack would not take no for an answer.

Despite his statements about "specific tastes" in which he pointed out our age gap, I knew there was something between us. First of all, I never kissed my friends like he'd just kissed me. Secondly, he had yet to let go of my hand. I had the strongest notion that what I was feeling wasn't one sided.

The first half of the walk back was in silence. It had been a world of relief to talk to someone, specifically Jack, about how my night had gone. Now on the walk back, the dread of how I'd find my parents when I got back was setting in. It appeared Jack was as lost in his thoughts as I was.

We were within about three houses of ours when Jack stopped us.

"Do you have a job or anything waiting on you when you get home?" he asked as he turned to face me.

"No, I need to find one," I answered. True to form, I added more information than was necessary. "I usually work for my father in the summers staging houses, but that's not an option this year."

"Would you like to stay here and be Josh's nanny? You don't have to decide now. You can sleep on it and let me know tomorrow."

"I don't know." I hadn't seen that coming at all.

"It would only be from now through the second week in August and, let's face it, we both know I need help with him."

"I don't have any place to stay," I pointed out.

Jack rubbed his thumb over the back of my hand as we spoke, but stopped over the silliness of my question. "You'd stay with us of course. It's a live-in position."

"You just met me this week." And, he was asking me to move in, a proposition that caused my head to spin.

"I only met his last nanny for thirty minutes before I hired her and, by the way, she stayed with us for five years."

"You are persistent."

"To a flaw, Caroline."

"Okay, I'll think on it."

"Good. It was Josh's idea and he will be over the moon. He adores you, you know."

It was after 11:00 p.m. when I walked back in the house. Chris and Becky were gone, but I found Bailey asleep in her bed next to mine. I couldn't believe they'd left her. I couldn't believe Becky had left her, but I'd never been so relieved to see Bailey. Chris was dragging Becky to their room when I walked out.

I saw the light from my parents' room shining under the door. I knocked lightly and was admitted in by my mother's muffled voice.

My father was sleeping soundly, but my mother was still up reading. I took a seat on the edge of her side of the bed and faced her.

"I see they left Bailey." I stated with the unspoken question of how did that happen.

"Yeah," my mother exhaled and laid her book across her lap. "Becky thought she'd punish us by taking Bailey, but your brother finally..."

"Grew a pair." I finished her sentence for her.

"I do not appreciate the language that's been used in this house tonight! I know it might not be mine much longer, but as long as it is, you'll watch your mouth, Caroline."

My mother had always been a stickler for our tone and our words and she was never one to allow us to scream at one another. We had thrown caution to the wind during our family brawl tonight and used words that Mother deemed unfit for her ears.

"Yes, ma'am." I paused as Daddy shifted his position. Both Mother and I had kept the conversation to a whisper as not to wake him.

"Not that it is any of your business," Mama began to elaborate, "but your brother told his wife that if she didn't get in the car right then she would need to call a cab to get back to Atlanta and it would be on her dime. I think he was fed up with her treating all of us the way she does."

"I can't believe you and Daddy have subsidized them all these years and this is how she acts toward you."

"Well, that's come to an end and she thought she'd punish us by taking Bailey, but Chris put his foot down."

"That's long overdue."

Mama picked up an envelope from the bedside table and laid her book in its place. "Here." She held it out for me. "This is for you."

The envelope had my name on the outside. I took it and opened it and found a check made out to me for $400. It was from Chris and Becky's account.

"What's this?" I studied it and was mystified as to why they had left a check for me and for that amount of money.

"Your father told Chris whatever he typically paid for Bailey's childcare he needed to pay you since you'd basically been in charge of Bailey all week long," Mama explained. She might have just scolded me over my use of words, but in that moment she had the tone of the cat that ate the canary.

I had to ask, "And he did it? Becky let him?"

"Becky was waiting in the car when that exchange took place. Chris made out the check and didn't bat an eye. I think he felt ashamed of the way Becky treated you and he'd had enough."

"So this is his way of buying me off?"

"CC just take the money or send it back." That cat versus canary voice was gone.

"I can't accept it."

It was tempting to keep it, but it just didn't seem right. It did remind me that I needed to tell Mama and Daddy about Jack's offer and I figured I might as well start with her. Plus, I was dying to tell someone.

Mama put her reading glasses on top of her book on the nightstand and began undressing out of her housecoat. I suppose she thought our conversation was over, but it wasn't.

"Jack offered me a job," I started.

"Really?" Mama was intrigued.

"As the nanny for Josh. Just until school starts."

My mother then had a slew of questions that I didn't have answers to yet like, "How much will you get paid? What are your hours? What will your duties include? Will you be responsible for driving the child around?"

The one question she asked that I could answer involved my living arrangements. "He knows you can't live here, right?"

"Yes, ma'am."

"So where will you live?" I think she knew the answer before she even asked the question.

"With him and Josh. I'll have my own room and bathroom and it's on a separate floor of the house from his and Josh's," I explained to her.

"CC, we all know there's something going on between the two of you so let me just clear up something, there's no way I will ever be okay with you living with a man out of wedlock let alone one that you only met six days ago. Make your own decisions, but just know that you are a reflection on how I raised you and that's not how I raised you."

"Yes, of course and I promise, it's just a job. There is some sort of pull toward him, but despite what you saw this afternoon, I'm not his type." I didn't dare tell her about the game or his specificities.

"You need to keep in mind that if you take this job, it is not about you. It is about that little boy. For his sake, and your own, you need to be careful not to get too attached. I know you, CC, and you need to guard your heart on this one. I've seen you with boys and I know you can handle yourself in that regard, but I've seen you with children, too, and..."

"I know, Mama. I know."

"I'm serious, CC, this isn't one of the children you are used to. No mother is going to come home when you leave. You may be filling a void for him and you need to be careful that he doesn't get too attached either."

"Okay, I really hadn't thought of it like that."

"You should."

"Mama, I might be good for him and I think this will be good for me."

"You're twenty-two years old. I can't make your decisions for you and you know what's right and wrong. You also know when you need to report to Mercer and you better have your head on straight because law school is some serious business." Mama motioned for me to get up. "We can talk about this more tomorrow. Go to bed."

The next morning, Mama insisted that I tell Daddy my news.

"Are you sure about this, CC? You just met him. You don't know him and you're going to go live..."

I stopped Daddy. "At dinner you had nothing but positive things to say about him."

"That's before I knew you were thinking of moving in with him."

"I'm not moving in with him. Well, I mean, I kind of am, but not like *that*." I didn't want to be brutally honest with them and explain that I just wasn't that lucky.

Daddy threw up his hands, exasperated. "I'm no longer in a position to provide your finances and you're a grown woman so I can't really tell you what to do."

Bailey walked in and the conversation was tabled.

While Mama put the finishing touches on breakfast, Bailey and I rushed out to set up the tent. Little did Bailey know that was my bait for luring Jack and Josh to us. Bailey and I agreed to put up the tent and our beach stuff, eat breakfast and then help Mama with the final touches of packing. Mama told us we could go on out to the beach, but we refused to go without her.

"Our last day at the beach will be spent with all of us at the beach!" I declared. "Together."

"That includes you, too, Granddaddy!" Bailey ran and jumped in his arms.

After breakfast Bailey and I packed our room.

"Aunt CC, is this our last day at the beach ever?" Bailey asked as she gathered her stuffed animals.

"No, but it might be our last day at this house. And that's okay." I tried to put a positive spin on the situation for her.

"But I like this house." Tears filled Bailey's eyes.

I stopped what I was doing, and took a seat on the bed and pulled Bailey into my lap. "You know, there are bigger, nicer houses out there that we could stay in. You should see Josh and Mr. Jack's house. It has two sets of stairs and, at the top, there's a room like a crow's nest on the mast of a pirate ship. The ceiling retracts and you can see all the stars in the sky. It's amazing. We might could find an amazing house like that to stay in one day."

"I guess, but I think this house is amazing," Bailey sniffled.

"You know what makes this house amazing?" I smiled.

"What?"

"You. So no matter what house we stay in, as long as you are there, it will be perfect." I started to tickle Bailey and I achieved my goal of lifting her spirits.

"And Bailey, just because Grandma and Granddaddy are selling this house doesn't mean we can't come back to the beach. Okay?"

"Okay." Bailey wrapped her arms around my neck and squeezed until I almost couldn't breathe.

Just before 11:00 a.m., Bailey pointed out the living room window toward the water and started to squeal, letting me know putting up the tent had worked.

"Aunt CC, Josh and Mr. Jack are outside! They're putting their chairs with ours."

I kept my cool and my mother, who was helping me pack all of our family photos, cut her eyes at me.

"There's not much more if you girls want to go on out. I can finish and join y'all in a few minutes," Mama offered.

"No, if it's only a few more minutes then we will stay and help and we'll all go out together. In fact, Bailey, start packing the cooler while Grandma and I finish."

Bailey did like she was asked and started emptying the contents of the refrigerator as I had second thoughts. "Bailey, run tell Mr. Jack and Josh that we will be right out. Then, come back and finish the cooler."

"Yes, ma'am." Bailey did not have to be asked twice. Out the door she went.

"It's good to make 'em wait every now and then." Mama patted my arm and gave me a wink.

"But it's good to be considerate, too."

By the end of the afternoon Mama and Daddy had thoroughly grilled Jack about the nanny position. They were subtle, but thorough all the same.

Around 3:00 p.m. my parents offered to take Bailey and Josh to get ice cream. Jack agreed that Josh could go. Perhaps he figured if they were to trust him with their child, adult or not, for the rest of the summer, he could trust them with his for a few minutes. After the okay was given, my parents left toward the public beach entrance with the two children skipping along in front of them. I know they missed Chris, but this was one of the happiest days they'd had at the beach in a long time.

"Let's get in the water." Jack stood and offered his hand to me.

"Race you to the sand bar."

I jumped up and ran. Jack chased after me. He caught me and grabbed me around the waist then hoisted me in the air. I screamed and he threw me like we'd thrown the kids earlier in the week. Had I not been flying through the air set to crash in the waves, I would have been turned on by his strength. I screamed just like the children did and popped up from the water laughing just like they did, too.

Jack and I waded the rest of the way to the sandbar laughing the whole time. It was fifteen or twenty yards to the person closest to us so we were basically alone with one another as we sat. This was probably my favorite place on Earth and my favorite thing to do, aside of my new found favorite of kissing Jack. I loved sitting and floating with the waves gently floating me backward and forward. The experience was made better only by having Jack there with me.

For once in my life I understood the draw of attraction to someone. I'd never thought of myself as pretty or beautiful so I never understood why men would fall all over themselves looking at me. But now, I found myself in their situation with Jack. I tried not to be one of the herds that salivated over him but I could hardly help myself.   Time and again, he'd nearly caught me memorizing the contours of his face, his arms, shoulders, back and every other part of him.   I could not imagine leaving him yet, not if I didn't absolutely have to.

"Does your dad quiz all of your potential employers to this extent?"   Jack's tone was playful, but I was a bit embarrassed none the less.

"Only the ones the whole family witnesses me kissing."

"Point taken."

Chapter 9

"How did it go with closing up the house and seeing your parents off?" Jack asked as he carried in my suitcases.

"It wasn't as bad as I thought it was going to be."

I followed him up the wide steps that led to a front porch spanning the entire façade of the house. It was a huge house, but simple, like an extra-large cottage. A house this size in Atlanta would have been far from anything that resembled a cottage.

"My parents packed the car last night so we were up and out in a flash this morning," I continued. "My father was determined to cut short the goodbyes and save any of us crying over the place one second more than we already had."

"Your father sounds like a smart man." Jack held the door.

I gave pause as I navigated the doorway. It was more than crossing the threshold that got me; it was the thought of all that had gone on with my father in the last six months. I answered slowly. "He is."

Jack noticed my hesitation. "Why did your family sell the house?"

"Why does anyone sell? The time's right. The offer's right," I shrugged.

Jack took a turn into the first doorway to the right and I followed. He flopped my bags down on the queen size bed that was the center of the room. The room was huge and evidently the one he intended to be mine. It had windows that looked out to the front porch. The whole place was open and airy. It was no less than four times the size of my bedroom at home. I'd never had a room right on the front of the house before and for precaution I've never rented a ground floor apartment in college either. In a place like this, in a gated beachfront community, I supposed it was as safe as any.

"So, what's the real reason?" Jack stepped away from the bed, but not toward me.

I sat the rest of my belongings on the bed with the rest, my travel case and purse. I gathered my nerves. I hated explaining to the owner of this grand house that my family was broke. What would he take me for? A gold digger? I wasn't. I was nothing like my sister-in-law. I didn't care about his money, but the story I was about to tell would make it seem like I should. If I wanted to continue a life of comfort the likes of which I'd been raised, I'd better find a man like him to latch onto.

"Before I tell you, you must promise you won't think any less of me," I begged.

Jack looked at me, his blue eyes growing bigger with curiosity.

"Promise," I glared at him.

"I promise," Jack replied.

I pushed the suitcases and other bags back from the edge of the bed and took a seat. Jack chose to stand. I ran my hands through my hair and dreaded spilling the tale. As much as I didn't want him to think me a gold digger, I didn't want him to think my father was a fool either. I told Jack what the fight was about last night, Becky's accusations about my father losing the family fortune, but I hadn't given him an exact account of how.

"My father owned one of the largest construction companies in Atlanta. He started off small, a few neighborhoods in up and coming areas around the metro area, then he took on a few office complexes. Things started to take off in the early seventies and by the late seventies he'd won bids to help with the skyscrapers that were going up. He made a killing and he was dang near famous. He rode out the storm that was the financial crisis of the Jimmy Carter era, the presidency, I mean, not when he was governor. Anyway, things kept up through the eighties. We didn't know all of this of course."

I fidgeted with the one ring I wore. I hadn't had it on all week so it was taking a little getting used to again. I hadn't had it long. It was a college graduation present from my parents. They didn't have the money to get me a car like they'd bought for Chris as his present, but this was more than good enough. It was the gold and diamonds of my grandmother's wedding set, melted down and made into what looked like a band of diamonds held together by a string of gold. My grandparents didn't have anything so her ring had tiny, flakes almost, of diamonds, nothing like the grand set my father gave my mother for their thirtieth anniversary.

"Anyway, a few years ago he decided to get out of the rat race. He wanted to go back to his roots, building houses. He bought some land out in Alpharetta, it's north of downtown and it was starting to boom. He wanted to slow down, move toward retirement, but not quit altogether. He took on a partner, one of our neighbors, Mr. Pole. He was an accountant."

Jack slumped down in a chair that sat in the corner near the front window. I suppose he didn't realize I was going to be so long winded about it. He listened attentively and hadn't lost interest yet.

"Mr. Pole invested money, but he syphoned far more than he invested. My father trusted him to pay the bills."

I covered my eyes and held my head in my hands. Through my fingers, I went on. "They were doing well at first and all of the money my father put in the business went toward the purchase of tracts of land. Mr. Pole's money was to go toward building materials. I don't understand the whole sorted scheme, but the short of it was that Mr. Pole put his money in long enough to show my father that it was there. He snatched it back out and used the credit of the company to buy supplies. When the houses sold he paid my father a draw and took one himself. Flim flam. Flim flam. He didn't pay the creditors. My father didn't know anything was wrong until the liens started showing up on homes at the closing table. It was a mess. Oh my God, just a mess. A colossal mess."

71

I glanced up at Jack and his mouth was dropped open and he was mid-exhale.

"I know. I know. The few people I've told ask the same thing, 'How did my father not know?' His area of expertise was building the houses and, again, he trusted his partner, a CPA, that he'd known for twenty years, to apply his expertise. He applied it alright."

"Luckily my parents' house in Atlanta is in my mother's name. I don't understand all of the whats, whys and hows, but everything in my father's name has to be liquidated to pay creditors. Mr. Pole used his expertise to cover his tracks. Somehow he has gotten off scott-free with the company money."

"I could go on, but part of the fight with Becky the other night was about her being bitter that my parents can't subsidize her lifestyle anymore. They're broke. Everything they'd worked so hard all their lives to accomplish is just gone, stolen, and there's nothing anyone can do about it."

I didn't know what else to say. I worried now what Jack would think of me. The one relief was that I appeared to be cried out over the subject. The two times I'd told the story to my best friends, I cried my eyes out. I felt so sorry for my parents. I felt the same for them, I just didn't have the tears anymore.

Jack straightened up in the chair from where he'd been slouching over his elbows on his knees. "Didn't you say you were going to law school? I'm guessing they can't help you with that now."

"Nope. I'm on my own. I don't mind. I'll figure it out somehow." I did my best to put on a brave face.

Jack walked over and took a seat on the bed next to me. "What are you going to do?"

"I've got a partial scholarship, so things could be worse." I didn't want our entire day to be clouded by the subject so I redirected us. "Plus, I've got this great job that I'm starting today and my boss, wow, he is a really great kisser."

Jack dropped his head as if embarrassed. "Ah, yes, about that. We should probably be a little hands off..."

"Whatever you say, Boss." I nudged him and gave him a half-hearted smile.

"CC, I hate that this has happened to your family. I wish I had some insightful wisdom to share. I mean, I think your parents are going to be okay and, from what I know of you, I think you're going to be just fine."

We sat there for a moment in silence, neither of us knowing what more could be added to my story that would make a difference.

"Do you mind if I use the chest of drawers? I don't have much, but I figure if I'm going to be here two months, I might put things away..."

"What's wrong, you don't like living out of a suitcase?" Jack laughed. "Of course you can use the chest of drawers. You can use anything in the house you like."

Another moment passed. I didn't want to get up and start unpacking with him sitting there.

"Daddy!" Josh called from the other end of the house.

"Ah, the DVD must have stopped," Jack stood, responding to the call of his son. He was almost out of the door when he turned and looked back at me. "Have I told you how glad I am to have you here?"

I was flattered. "No." I couldn't contain the grin on my face and the party going on inside of me. Butterflies on steroids or something were dancing in my stomach.

"I ran out of overnight diapers about two weeks ago and Josh wets the bed every night. I swear I haven't had a full night's sleep in over ten days."

"Oh, okay." That's not the reason I'd expected he was glad to have me there.

"I'm hoping you and I can work something out. Alternate nights or something. You change the bed one night and I'll get it the next. That way we are getting some sleep."

"Sure."

I saw that as a challenge. My mission would be to help Josh learn to sleep through the night without wetting the bed. If I could do that, then we'd all get a full night's sleep.

I called my mother that evening, after I knew they had enough time to get home. I told her what was going on and asked her how to train a child not to wet the bed. At first she razzed me about wanting to make brownie points with Jack, then she told me what I needed to do.

"Set a bed time. 8 or 8:30 for his age. Cut off liquids at 6:30 and, since you typically stay up until 11:00 or midnight, wake him up right before you go to bed and take him to the bathroom. Most children get up with the sun, so he'll make it. You'll see."

"Thanks, Mom. I'm hugging you through the phone."

"I'm hugging you back, Baby. Are you doing alright down there?"

"Yes, ma'am. I miss y'all, but other than that everything's going good." Things were fine. I was starting to love life again and so far I'd not felt any weirdness from Jack regarding my family's financial predicament.

For a week I followed my mother's advice to the letter about getting Josh to sleep through the night. Jack and Josh fought the bedtime every night. They both made the argument that it was summer and Josh should be able to stay up as late as he liked. I made my famous homemade chicken fingers for dinner one night. Our maid who worked part-time as a cook at a Black-Eyed Pea restaurant, taught me how to make them. I approached the subject again.

"If you ever want these chicken fingers again or any of my cooking, you two boys will come around to my way of thinking about a bedtime. I think 9:00 is fair." I didn't tell them that I also reset the obvious clocks to say

9:00 when it was really 8:30. "Would y'all like some homemade honey mustard?"

"You made homemade honey mustard?" Jack questioned.

"Yes." I passed him the glass jar I'd put it in.

"Son, we'll both be going to bed at 8:30 now." Jack said as he tasted his first bite of chicken dunked in the sauce. "CC, do you have any other demands?"

"Not right now," I replied. Another thing I didn't tell them was about the toilet training. As far as I'd told Jack, the bedtime was strictly for keeping Josh on a schedule, which was good for children.

I confessed fairly quickly to Jack about the clocks and he called me, "manipulative, but in a good way."

Everything was going great. We played in the surf most days. I cooked most of our meals. Jack was still hands off and I tried to respect that, but it didn't mean I wanted things that way. There was hardly a moment in the day that I didn't want to kiss him and more.

Josh went to bed without hassle almost every night at 8:30. That left Jack and I time to talk and get to know one another better. Jack and I usually turned in around 10:30. Sometimes, in the hours we had alone, we sat on the porch and listened to the tide. Other nights we watched TV and others we just talked and talked and talked. Every now and then, I'd find my fingers locked in Jack's or his arm around me.

On the second floor of the house there was a double chase lounge and, most nights when we sat on the deck, that's where we sat. Jack sat on the right and I sat on the left. The thing was huge and Josh could have easily sat between us and we would have all had room. We sat on that level of the house not because there was a better view of the ocean, but that's where Jack preferred to sit in case Josh called out from his sleep. Despite the way we met, him having lost Josh for more than an hour, I knew Jack was a good father. His attention to Josh made him all the more endearing.

I drew my knees up and sat on my hip, facing him. "Tell me about Josh's mother."

Jack turned and faced me the same. He studied me for a moment and I could see the wheels turning behind his eyes. The lack of pictures of her in the house told me there was a story. There was a story that was defined by more than the word "widower."

"Tell me the real story." I coaxed him.

Jack reached over and push a few stray hairs out of my face and tucked them behind my ear. "What makes you think..."

I cut him off and got to the point. "Why are there no pictures of her in the house, if not just for Josh's benefit?"

"You are very observant." It was not a compliment that he paid me, it was another stall.

"It's not observant to notice things that are obvious."

Jack straightened more and laid his left arm across the back of the chase. "Her name was Miriam and she got a blood clot right after Josh was born. It went to her brain and she died. It was that simple."

"If it's that simple then why not put out her photos? You must have some of her. What about your wedding photos? You must have some from..."

"Yes, there are photos, but why do you care?"

There was no more an easy answer to that question than the questions I was asking him apparently. I couldn't very well tell him that I was falling in love with him, with him and Josh and this life here with them. I wanted to know the woman I wanted to replace, that I was replacing.

I struggled to form an answer, but I managed. "I can't imagine growing up and not knowing my mother, not even seeing a picture of her. I guess I feel sorry for Josh and wonder what he thinks."

"Ah, so this is about Josh." Jack studied my face.

"Yes, and me. I'm curious." I was curious as to what would make Jack keep something so meaningful as a picture of his mother from Josh. "Why aren't there daily reminders of her? If I died tomorrow, I'd want there to be something to remind you of me even though..."

With offense in his voice, he bit out the words. "She wasn't like you."

I was taken aback and withdrew to the far side of the chase. Although I understood that was a slight against her, I'd never been praised in such a tone.

I didn't want this conversation to be so difficult. I wanted the truth, but I did not want him to resent me. I composed my response and delivered it with the intention of returning us to a lighter mood. "But you loved her and she was of your tastes." I cocked an eyebrow as I delivered the reminder.

Jack almost laughed. "You use my words against me at every opportunity."

I tilted my head, gave a shrug and smiled. "So?"

"You can look around here and tell that my family..."

"Yeah," I didn't let him say the words to point out their wealth. I got where he was going so we could move on.

"Miriam came from money as well. She and Leslie Daniel were very much alike in some regards. Anyway, I knew Miriam dated around, but I didn't know to what extent. She was a beautiful girl and she used her beauty to her advantage. She could charm the pants off of anyone."

"Including you?" I asked, an answer I didn't like to imagine.

"Of course, off of me, too."

"I took her to meet my parents. One look and..."

"And it wasn't about you anymore."

"Within a week she told me she was pregnant. I wasn't the only one she told. She phoned my mother with the joyous news."

I covered my mouth with both hands.

Jack reached over and took my hands in his. "You were so worried the other day that I'd think you were a gold digger when you told me about your parents. I could tell." Jack let out a sigh. "Oh, you silly girl, I couldn't spot one back then, but now I can, and, Caroline, you are not like that."

"What did your mother do?" I asked him quietly.

"She did the worst thing she could. She told my father."

Jack went silent, the events likely replaying in his head. I waited patiently.

When he began again, I learned more about him in that five minutes than I had in our entire time together. "My parents had always had big plans for me. For my mother I was to be the next president of her company, Belgrave Chocolates. I could repair every machine on the factory floor by the time I was fifteen. I know every recipe by heart the same way that I know how to tie my shoes or recite the books of the Bible. From the ground up, she made me learn every aspect."

"My father was a Senator and I was to take over his seat. He didn't just want me to be president of a chocolate factory. He wanted, excuse me, he wants me to be President of the United States. He couldn't have me refusing to marry a girl that had accused me of getting her pregnant. He couldn't afford the scandal. He didn't even bother to talk to me. He scheduled an engagement party and a wedding and the whole affair before I had time to really wrap my mind around what she'd told me, let along question her or try to figure out..."

"Oh, Jesus," I lowered my voice to the tiniest whisper. "Is Josh yours?"

"It doesn't even matter. It never has."

Jack wasn't just a good father. He was a great father.

Chapter 10

Each night I crept out of my bedroom between 11:00 p.m. and 1:00 a.m., tip-toed up the stairs, plucked Josh from his bed, carried him into the bathroom, squatted in front of him and helped him with his pajama bottoms. One night he might sit and another night he might stand. After he was finished, I carried him back to his bed and tucked him in again.

About three weeks into it, one night around 1:00 a.m. after a late night of talking on the phone to one of my friends back home, I stood Josh in front of the toilet as I usually did. I got down on my knees in front of him to help him with his shorts and as soon as the shorts went down he fire hosed me. The hot liquid hit me at the top of my right shoulder and left a slash of pee that went from my shoulder down and across my chest to my hip and back down and across to my knee. I screamed without the dampness even touching my skin.

That night I walked Josh back to bed to keep him from pressing into my wet clothes and getting him wet, too. With Josh tucked back in his bed and fast asleep, and thinking I was the only one up, I stripped out of my night shirt and shorts and carried them in my hand as I crept back downstairs. When I turned the corner I tossed them in the washing machine in the laundry room that was tucked under the stairs. I started down the path through the kitchen to the hall toward my room. I was wearing only my panties when I heard Jack.

"Caroline?"

He startled me. I should have run for my room, but instead I stood frozen. My feet were glued to the hardwoods where I'd first heard his voice.

Only the light above the sink was on in the whole house. It was Jack's custom to leave it on like a night light. There was a storm brewing so there was no moonlight seeping through the doors and windows. It was dark, but that little bit of light from the pendant above the sink was just enough to keep me from slipping away under the cover of darkness.

I was certain Jack was behind me. I knew he'd seen me, but how much he'd seen, I didn't know. What must he think I was doing tip-toeing around the house in the dark? I'd planned on telling him what I was up to with Josh and the bedwetting, but I hoped he'd notice and ask me.

"Jack?" I mirrored his question with my own.

"What are you doing?" I heard his footsteps behind me. What a time for him to finally ask.

"Wellllll..." I squared my shoulders and stood up straight.

"Are you..." Yes, he was going to ask if I was naked, but I didn't let him get that far.

I spotted Jack's dress shirt where he'd taken it off as soon as he walked in the door from a meeting in Pensacola just days before. It was still hanging over the back of one of the bar stools there in the kitchen. It was within arm's reach. Without turning around I grabbed it and slipped it on.

For the most part I was covered, my shoulders and breasts were, so I went ahead and turned around as I took one of the buttons in one hand and the other receiving end in the other. The shirt was still gaped open showing my bare skin from my neck to the top of my panties. Jack had seen all of those parts of me in a bathing suit so I didn't think much of it.

"The reason Josh hasn't been wetting the bed is because I get him up about this time every night and take him to use the restroom. Tonight he put the mark of Zorro on me in pee. I think it only got on my clothes, but..."

Jack came closer and closer as I spoke. I stopped talking and forgot about the buttons when I noticed the way he was looking at me. I'd seen that look before. It was that once over from head to toe and back again, slowly, just before he kissed me on the beach in front of the Daniels that afternoon. It was the way he looked at me the night when I'd had the fight with Becky. I knew that look. Tonight it was the look that let me know he was fighting the urge to forget our age difference and that I was now his employee. That was a fight I'd hoped he'd lose.

There he was in front of me, blue eyes blazing, bare chested, bare footed, in nothing but a pair of pajama pants, thin pajama pants, and about as erect as any man could be. "Caroline, are you trying to make me lose my mind?"

"No, I was trying to help you get a good night's sleep."

"Oh, dear girl," he inched closer, "There's more than one way to help a man get a good night's sleep."

My feet were no longer frozen. I took a step closer to him. Another step and I was within reach so I took that as well.

"I have some Tylenol PM in my purse if you need it." I draped my arms around his neck and as I did the shirt opened wide leaving me bare against him.

Jack stopped shy of wrapping his arms around me and rested his hands on my hips, but the cat had gotten his tongue.

"I'm guessing that's a 'no' to the Tylenol?" I commented.

I inched up on my toes and the friction of my bare nipples against the hair on his chest was like having them gently flicked at the same time by each hair they passed over. Shivers went down my legs and I let out a few ragged breaths.

It had been over a year since my last sexual encounter. Much more than a touch from him and I would come undone. I wondered if the same was true for him. I knew it had been at least four weeks for him because he'd hardly been away from me long enough to accomplish it with anyone else. I wondered if he revved his own engine, but had no way of knowing. Maybe all it would take was a few touches for him as well.

I held firm on my toes. I could feel his hard-on against my belly.

"Bend your knees." I let the words slide out of my mouth and over his neck. I could feel the chills spring up on his skin.

"What?" he asked with a ragged breath.

"Bend...your...God damn...knees..." I did it again about as sultry as I could manage without thinking myself ridiculous.

Jack did as I commanded and I tilted my hips away as he did. The thin pajama pants were not enough to hold him up right and I had counted on that. He dropped at just the right angle to fall between my legs. Still on my toes, I stepped to him, dragging myself over him as I went.

For once, I used the pelvic hug to my advantage. It was that thing perverts did when they hugged me. They dipped their knees and dropped their dicks between my legs for that little something extra. Normally, I hated it, but tonight, I loved it.

The thin material of my panties and his pants were not enough to keep him from parting me ever so slightly as I glided over him. When my pelvic bone met his a shiver ran through me. Jack was so long his tip went all the way to a place between my butt cheeks.

The heat was rising in both of us. I could tell by his gasp that I wasn't alone in this.

Jack held on tight, fingers squeezing into to each of my hips, as I moved back and then over him again.

"What are you doing?"

"Wait for it." I whispered against his skin once more.

"Oh, God, are you trying to..." He took a breath between each word. I could feel him quaking a little beneath me. He didn't push me away or pull back.

Over him I went again. Each time I ground my chest up and down him as I slid back and forth. It didn't take many passes over him before he clinched on tight and when he did it parted me a little more, hitting that spot and ringing that bell within me. It wasn't a loud bell, just enough to send a little vibrations, and give me what I'd been aching for since I met him. It was just enough to take the edge off.

If he could give me an orgasm from just this, what could he do if he really put his mind to it? He could ravage me. That's what he could do. He'd told me so.

As I thought about Jack's potential, he gave two quick jerks and I knew mine wasn't the only bell that had been rung.

"Oh, God, Caroline," so quietly, he said my name.

"Sleep well, Boss."

I kissed him on the cheek and turned around so quickly that he still didn't have a chance to get a full frontal look at me. I slinked out of his shirt and let if fall behind me as I walked away.

When I got to the door of my room, I looked over my shoulder to see Jack still standing there watching me. "Just remember, Boss, I have youth on my side so it might be me that ravages you." I blew him a kiss, went in my room and shut the door.

The next morning Jack was up and gone before I woke. I knew this because of the way Josh came bouncing into bed with me to wake me up. At first I was disappointed that Jack was gone until I found a note on the kitchen island.

CC,

Willie Wonka, that's me, has gone to the office today. I've been summoned. Have fun at the beach with Josh. I'll be home for dinner, but don't go to any trouble on my account.

Thanks for last night. I slept great!

-Jack

83

PS
Keep the shirt. I'll never be able to wear it again without getting hard.

I squealed and Josh came running. I folded the note and shoved it between the folds of the shirt. Josh was six and he could read already. I didn't need him getting a look at what his father wrote and have to explain what "getting hard" meant.

"Are you okay?!!" he yelled.

"Super!" I yelled back as I picked him up and spun him around.

"Put me down!" Josh screamed.

"Nope! I'm gonna fly you to the moon!"

"Not to the moon!!! I hate space!" Josh screamed with all of his might.

I promptly sat him down. "What do you mean you hate space?" I asked calmly. "You have an observatory on top of your house. You can't hate space."

Josh's eyes got big. I'd used a word that was too big, "observatory."

"Never mind," I said. "Do you like camping?"

He twisted his head like he was about to shake it in the negative.

"Oh stop." I slapped my forehead. "You've never been camping?"

Josh rolled his eyes, to him the answer was obvious and I was just silly for asking.

"Well, we are going to fix that! We are sleeping under the stars tonight."

I loaded Josh in the car and we went to find sleeping bags. I figured that was a better idea than Jack's. There was no way I was getting a mattress of any size up the stairs by myself and I wanted this all worked out by the time Jack got home.

84

Once back at the house, Josh and I went out to the water for a little while. I didn't really know when to expect Jack, but I wanted dinner ready when he arrived so around four we came in and I started preparations. I didn't have a real campfire, but the grill did the trick for my Campfire Chicken recipe, carrots, potatoes, chicken quarters, some seasonings, some water and butter, all sealed in a tin-foil pouch and shoved in the hot coals. In this instance, they would have to be shoved on top of a rack in the gas grill. It would taste the same and be called the same and it was the best I could do for our first, kind-of, sort-of, camping trip.

It always took a while for that chicken to cook so I didn't worry when it was almost six and Jack still wasn't back. It was close to 7:00 when the chicken was finally done and that's when I started to worry about him. I hadn't heard a word all day. The two days he'd gone to the office before he'd called and checked in on Josh. There was no call today. Josh didn't notice anything more than his growling stomach. I'd held him off of snacks because I didn't want to ruin his appetite. He was starving so at 7:00 I let him go ahead and eat. I went ahead and ate with Josh because everything I'd done that day was about Josh and I didn't see the need to stop then.

After Josh finished eating, I ushered him into the shower and I ran down to my room and got mine at the same time. Once we were done, I took Josh up to the top floor. I hadn't let him go up there all day so he had no idea what awaited him. While he was in the shower I ran up there and pressed the button that opened the roof. I stole a couple of candles from the downstairs décor and lit them.

When Josh topped the stairs, I announced, "Welcome to our campout!"

"This isn't the woods," Josh quickly pointed out.

"It is if you pretend and we are sleeping under the night sky."

The look on his tiny face was sheer joy. For just a second, I got a glimpse of his father in his eyes. No one knew if he was really Jack's son, but there was a glimmer. Jack was right, though, it didn't matter. What I saw in him was joy, a rare thing for the Belgrave boys, but there it was.

The boards creaked like those in an old house. Someone was on the staircase. I hadn't heard the door or him call our names, but when I looked toward the stairwell, there he was. It was Jack. Beautiful, fun to look at, Jack.

It was too hot for the sleeping bags so we'd opened them up and I put a bed sheet out for each of us. Josh and I had just crawled in when Jack appeared.

"Hey! What are you guys doing?" Jack crawled across the floor toward Josh.

"We're camping out!" Josh replied, giddy to share the experience with his father.

Jack smiled at me and mouthed the words, "Thank you."

"Dinner's in the oven, grab some then get a shower and come join us," I told him.

"Okay and, Josh, I brought you something." Jack rubbed him on the head and then stood to leave. "I'll give it to you when I come back."

"Hurry, Daddy!"

"I'll be back before you know it."

Jack came back carrying a box, about the size that reams of paper came in when they were shipped to my dad's office.

"What is it?" Josh's eyes grew wide. One would have thought it was Christmas morning.

Jack sat the box down in front of him. "I'm sorry I was so late getting home. I had to drive all the way to far side of Tallahassee for this. Two and a half hours each way, plus I did stop by my office and I ran into my father."

"Why Tallahassee?" I inquired.

"It's home when we aren't here." Jack explained as he pulled out a pocket knife

"Oh." I watched vacantly while Josh salivated over what might be in the box and Jack cut it open.

As soon as the tape was slit, Josh lifted the lid. I was just about as curious as he was about what was inside. It wasn't a toy and his face went blank. He pulled out a photo frame as he glanced to his father for answers. From where I sat, the box looked to be filled with them.

"This is Mommy," Jack told him, "and you can put these up in your room if you like. One or all of them, as many as you like. They belong to you."

"Mommy?" Josh stared at the picture. I would have stared, too, but from my vantage point all I saw was the back of the frame.

"You've been asking about her for so long I figured..." Jack stuttered. He was searching for ways to explain to the child why now.

I ran interference for Jack. "Josh, can I see?" I reached out for the photo. "I bet she was pretty."

I don't know what I expected, but the woman in the photo was not it. Maybe I expected her to look like me. She didn't. She had red hair. She had brown eyes. Maybe I knew too much about her to think she was attractive at all. Nothing that I saw in the photo appealed to me. The description Jack had given of her character colored everything I saw in the photograph. Josh took out one after another and not a one of them inspired me to think warm and fuzzy thoughts about her, but I faked it for Josh's sake.

"I think you have her eyes," I told him and that was true.

With the exception of his hair color, Josh was Miriam made over. Thank God for the brown hair he got from Jack or whomever.

Jack sucked up all of his animosity toward the woman in the photographs and followed my lead. As we sat under the stars, he told Joshua only good stories about his mother. It was sweet and selfless. It was what a real parent does.

That night I fell asleep beneath the stars with the man I loved and a little boy whose heart was so full of love it was about to burst as he lie between us. The both of them held my heartstrings in palm of their hands.

Chapter 11

Staying with Jack and Josh I'd lost all sense of time. I knew days were turning into weeks and time was passing, but if asked what the date was, I was at a loss.

Josh took his breakfast to the T.V. room and sat watching cartoons. The boy ate as much bacon as a grown man and, that morning, I had to hold him off so there would be some for Jack when he came down. He would have eaten the entire package if I had let him.

I waited to eat with Jack and over breakfast with me at the kitchen island Jack mentioned that his parents were arriving the next afternoon. That news caught me completely off guard. I didn't ask why they were coming out loud, but it was written all over my face.

"They're coming in for the fourth." A few swallows of orange juice later and Jack added, "I'm sure I mentioned it."

"And today is?" I asked.

"The second."

"Oh, crap!" I nearly choked on my pancakes. "I've got to clean this entire place in one day?"

"Why? Are you one of those women that picks up before the housekeeper comes so they won't judge you? My mother used to do that. It always boggled my mind. Why have a cleaning crew if..."

"You have a cleaning crew?" I was dumbfounded.

"Yes, they come every Thursday afternoon." Jack continued eating as if there wasn't a thing out of the ordinary. "We're usually at the beach while they're here."

"Do you know I've been sneaking around stripping beds, doing mine and Josh's laundry and cleaning everything else when y'all aren't looking?" I held my head in my hands. "And you have a cleaning crew? I guess they must love the shit out of me! I even dusted the baseboards yesterday morning."

"You what? Why would you think you needed to do that?" Jack put his fork and knife down. He'd been laughing until my baseboard comment.

"First of all I saw they needed to be done, so I did them. Second, you are paying me..."

"I'm paying you to help me look after Josh, entertain him a little and make sure he doesn't escape. So you've been cleaning this entire place, cooking all of our meals and looking after Josh, which includes staying up until all hours of the night training him not to wet the bed?" Most people would have been pleased with all of that, but Jack didn't sound pleased. Our morning appeared to have taken a very serious turn.

Sheepishly, I answered, "Yes."

"Good, God! What are you some sort of superwoman?" I didn't have a chance to answer, not that I would have, because Jack stood up from the table and left. "Wait right here," he told me as he walked away.

"Okay?" I had no idea if he was mad with me or not and where it was going, but I did as he said. I waited.

Jack returned with his checkbook and pen in hand. He sat back down and pushed his plate to the side. "We need to renegotiate."

"Excuse me?" This whole conversation was becoming more and more confusing.

"I've been paying you $250 per week and that was just for looking after Josh. How much do I owe you for the rest?" He put the pen to the paper and waited.

"Nothing."

Jack raised his eyes and met mine, staring at me, waiting for me to give him a figure.

I began again after gathering my nerves. It was no secret I needed the money, but I didn't feel right about taking it. "I can't take your money anymore."

"What? Why not?" Jack was stunned. "Are you quitting?"

"No! I mean, not unless you want me to. I don't want to quit."

"Then what' the problem?"

"I can't take your money anymore."

"Why the Hell not?"

For someone who was really bright, I was going to have to spell it out for him.

"I can't take your money after the good night sleep incident. There's a word for girls that…"

"Oh, Jesus Christ, Caroline! Two separate issues!"

I looked at him blankly, determined not to budge.

"Just so you know," Jack ran a hand through his hair and that alone was enough to make me sure I was doing the right thing, "I would never pay for that and I'm confident you'd never…" He stopped and didn't complete his sentence. He just shook his head and started making out the check.

"You can waste your time writing that if you want, but I'll never cash it!" I grabbed our plates and started for the sink with them.

Jack put the pen down. "What do you want then?"

"Do you consider us friends?" I asked him from the other side of the kitchen island.

"Of course we are. So as your friend, I'm going to help you look after your son this summer and in exchange you are going to let me rent that guest room from you." I nodded toward my room.

I continued and Jack listened attentively. "I like cooking so I'll continue doing the cooking."

"Good. I like your cooking and so does Josh. I fear he's becoming spoiled, but I can live with it as long as you make the homemade chicken fingers for him regularly." Jack was starting to tease me again.

"Anyway. In exchange for me cooking the majority of the week, you can pick up to-go or take Josh and I out to dinner occasionally. We could ride bikes up to Goatfeathers. Josh would love that, and it's only right up the street."

"What if I have terms of my own?" Jack made his way around the island to where I was loading the dishwasher.

"Feel free, it's your house, just know I won't take your money other than to buy groceries for the house or something like that."

Jack stepped close to me, closing the gap between us. "Your terms are fine, but I don't want you cleaning the house anymore. I have people for that and you don't need to worry with it. If you think they need to do a better job, then I'll take that up with them."

I smiled, diverting my eyes away from Jack. "Okay."

I went to wipe the hair from my eyes and Jack caught my hand. "About the good night sleep incident as you called it. Tell me," he hesitated. Taking a hard look at me, searching my face, Jack thought better of asking the question. "Never mind."

I had a feeling I knew what he was asking. "No, I don't do *that* to my friends."

Thank goodness Jack didn't press me further and try to make me define what I thought we were because all of this was new to me. I either had boyfriends or I didn't. I never had this in between stuff or this waiting or game playing or whatever it was. This was foreign to me and I would be the last one to be able to put a label on it.

That afternoon Jack and I sat in our beach chairs. We each had a book in our hands and we were both watching Josh make new friends and play at the edge of the water. It was getting late in the afternoon when I looked up from my book and spotted Josh about ten yards down the beach. He was talking with Leslie Daniel and her grandfather.

"Jack." I reached over and took his hand.

Jack lifted his eyes from his book and glanced my way.

92

"Josh is about ten yards to your right. He's talking to your stalker." I teased him and he didn't think it was nearly as funny as I did.

Jack gave me a chastising look. "She's not stalking me."

"Really?" I challenged. "She walks just this far up the beach and turns around every day. She checks to see if you're out. I can't believe you haven't noticed."

Jack let out a huff. "Let me go retrieve him."

"Shall I come with you?" I laid my book down and reached for my hat.

"Nah. I got him."

"Okay." Jack started away. I didn't let him get too far, only a few steps, before I called out to him. "Hey, Jack, if I catch her looking this way, you better be looking, too, or she'll think I'm blowing her a kiss." I bit my lip, wrinkled my nose and smiled at him.

"You are shameful!" Jack tried not to laugh as he made his way through the sand.

It was ten minutes before Jack and Josh came back and I did blow him that kiss while he was over there.

Once back at the tent, Jack started packing up. He had Josh gathering his toys and saying his good-byes. "CC, what's the most extravagant thing to know how to cook?"

"Excuse me?" I asked.

"We're having dinner guests."

I knew immediately what had happened, not how, but definitely what. "Nooooo." I drew out the word as I dug my feet in the sand.

"Come on now. Be a sport." Jack grabbed my hand and pulled me up.

"Fine. We need to go to the grocery store."

"What do you have in mind?"

"You'll have to wait and see. Plus, we need to pick up some things to have on hand for your parents coming."

Jack and I worked together to take down the tent. I carried it up and he got the cooler and chairs. Josh trailed behind us with his toys.

On the brief walk up to the house Jack asked me, "CC, do you want to go home to Atlanta to be with your family for the fourth?"

I thought about my answer and didn't respond until I came to the bottom step of the porch. I leaned the tent against the lowest rail and answered, "I guess there'd be no point. I spoke with my mother on the phone about coming home two nights ago. I offered and she said I might as well stay here if I wanted to. She didn't want my fourth to be ruined like everyone else's had been."

"What do you mean 'ruined'?" he asked as he came up the steps with the cooler.

"My family always came to our beach house for the fourth and now..."

Jack didn't make me finish. "I see."

We started up the steps to the porch and I felt obligated to ask, "Do you mind if I stay here? I'm sorry I didn't think to ask before when you told me about your parents coming. I don't want to hone in or be in the way or anything."

Josh was ahead of us and wandered on inside. Jack instructed him to go get in the shower and change clothes before he responded to me. "You can invite your parents to come here if you like. I can call my parents and tell them not to come."

I gasped. "No! You can't tell your parents they can't come to their own house because of me. Don't be ridiculous!"

"I'm not being ridiculous and this is my house so I can..."

I felt silly. I'd just assumed it was their house. I cut Jack off anyway. "It's not necessary. Really. Plus, after the way things went with Chris and Becky at the beach house this summer." I shrugged. I contemplated how to word what I was feeling before coming out with it.

"Of course I would love to see my parents, but I think my family needs to start making new traditions."

"So, you're staying here? With us?" Jack asked.

"As long as you'll have me."

That evening, the Daniels were fashionably late. I thought it was inconsiderate, but I didn't let it phase me. I'd pulled out all the stops on dinner and on the way I looked.

I'd picked up a dress in one of the new boutiques in Seaside earlier in the week. I knew I shouldn't spend money on frivolous things like dresses since my parents explained I'd have to pay my own way through law school, but I sprang for it when I saw it hanging in the window. It might as well have had my name on it.

The front of the top of it looked like a strapless bustier made of white raw silk and the back was a ribbon woven through eyelets down each side and tied in a bow at the top. I knew when I bought it that I'd never get it tied without help. I bought it anyway.

The skirt was made of a flowing gauze or organza type material over an equally flowing slip and it went all the way to the floor. The overlay had tiny silver flowers embroidered in it. The whole dress was a contradiction. I couldn't decide if it was formal or casual or what, but I wore it anyway. I loved it. I loved the way I felt when I saw myself in the mirror and I loved the idea that it might keep Jack from being able to take his eyes off of me that night.

Once my makeup was complete, I pulled my hair up in a loose bun and slipped on the dress. I was right about needing help to tie the back. As hard as I tried, it was no use. I wandered barefoot down the hall toward the kitchen while holding up my top. As I passed through the kitchen toward the living room I called for Jack just in time to see him coming down the stairs.

I don't know if he had put the thought into his looks the way I'd put into mine, but if Jack hadn't then he fooled me. He was wearing a white linen button up shirt that was open at the top allowing a glimpse of his chest hair. He paired the shirt with khaki slacks and they fit him like the ones Matthew McConaughey wore in the movie A Time To Kill. His hair was still damp from his shower and it begged me to run my fingers through it.

I don't know if I had a look that gave me away, but Jack had a look. That heated look he got and the up and down way his eyes drug over me, I'd seen it a few times before and there it was again. Jack froze on the staircase and gave me that look. When he finally spoke, only the word, "Hey," slipped passed his lips.

"Hey." I replied.

Maybe I had that look too. For a moment we were both stuck. Perhaps we were both wondering what to do about the other, both of us fighting the urge that was pulling us together. Maybe he was fighting that urge to ravage me. I hoped he was and I still hoped that was a fight he would eventually lose.

Jack took two steps and it freed my feet from their planted spot on the floor.

"Can you help me with this?" I asked as I turned around, revealing the back.

"Oh, uh..." There was a clonking noise and Jack shouting behind me "Shit!"

I jerked back around to see Jack stumbling to catch himself at the bottom of the stairs. I held my top up with one hand and reached out to help him with the other, all the while laughing.

"I'm sorry," I continued to giggle. I was sorry for laughing, but couldn't help myself.

Once we both regained our composure, I turned around and Jack took the two ends of the ribbon in his hands. He pulled them so tight that it forced my breasts together and I bulged at the top. I was never at a shortage for cleavage, but this was almost indecent.

"Umm, I hate to complain, but I'm going to need you to loosen the reigns a little." I blamed it on not being able to breathe.

"Sorry." Jack gave it another shot. "How's that?"

I looked down at my chest. The twins were still out on the front porch, but they didn't look like they were about to go for a run in the yard now. "Better."

When the Daniels finally showed up, around 7:20, they weren't much more than background noise for the evening Jack and I had. For dinner I served a cracked black pepper crusted beef tenderloin, twice baked potatoes, steamed broccoli, Caesar salad, yeast rolls and a chocolate silk pie for dessert, but I wasn't showing off for them. Jack might have wanted me to show off for them, but all of my efforts were for him. From dinner to the small talk I made with them to ignoring the jabs Leslie and her grandmother took at me, all the while thinking they were over my head, it was all to please him. Pulling out my chair for me, standing each time I left the table to retrieve something for our guests, who did seem bent on running me like a server, a hand under the table and on my thigh as he ate, helping me clear the plates when everyone was finished eating, telling me to leave the plates in the sink and he'd help me clean up later, placing a hand on the small of my back when he led us into the living room after dinner, all of those things gave me hope that I was succeeding. I hoped the sum of all of the little gestures were proof that we were past just trying to keep Leslie Daniel at bay. Leslie wasn't there for all of our private moments over the last few weeks, when he had no reason to act, and I took comfort in that fact.

At 8:30, Jack escorted Josh up to bed, but not before Josh kissed me goodnight and hugged me like there was no tomorrow. "Good night, sweet boy," I whispered in his ear so that only he could hear me. For a moment, I forgot my mother's warning and then it jumped to the forefront of my mind. I came close to telling Josh that I loved him, but I held back.

As Jack started up the stairs carrying a very tired Josh in his arms, Mr. Daniel excused himself to the restroom. I heard each step Jack took on the stairs. I heard him hit the landing at the top and so did Mrs. Daniel and Leslie.

"You look remarkably young, dear. Would you mind sharing with us just how old you are?" dripping with sweetness, Mrs. Daniel asked.

Leslie leaned in for the answer, but I didn't give them the one they were seeking.

"A lady never tells." I smiled politely and prayed Jack would be back soon.

The niceties fell by the wayside. "Now look here, honey child, I don't know what you think you are doing..."

"Would you ladies care for some coffee?" I stood from my seat on the couch and walked to the kitchen.

The two women huffed in unison. They followed me, but had the good grace to keep the kitchen island between us as I set about working the coffee maker.

"You know, Grandmother," Leslie gazed at her nails, pretending not to care, "my feathers are not ruffled at all. Jackson's mother will put an end to this as soon as she arrives tomorrow."

"Oh, you're probably right, maybe we should go so you can start packing your bags, dear," Mrs. Daniel followed her granddaughter's lead.

"Don't let the door hit you," I said under my breath.

"What did you say?" Leslie's head nearly spun off her shoulders.

"Sorry, I'll speak up. Cream or sugar?" I turned and reached for the canister on the counter behind me.

"That's not what you said!" Leslie snapped.

Leslie and her grandmother failed to realize I grew up with a pack of snobby, mean girls so this wasn't my first trip to the rodeo. I knew ignoring her was my best option so I turned around in my own good time. The coffee was barely dripping when I removed the pot and held the cup under. Once the cup was full I replaced the pot and slid the cup over to Leslie.

"Black it is." I felt my face would crack if I smiled any bigger.

"Now look here!" Mrs. Daniel leaned across the island.

I applied the same technique to dealing with Mrs. Daniel. "Black as well. I hope you like it." My face was definitely going to crack.

"Oh, yes, mark my words, you'll be out with the other trash when his mother and father arrive tomorrow." Mrs. Daniel scowled.

"Since you are Hell bent on giving me something to worry about, let me give you a little something, too." I leaned over and adjusted my boobs within the top of my dress. When I stood back up the twins were damn near about to escape.

Leslie was flat as a pancake and her grandmother's had fallen victim to gravity long ago so I enlightened them on the joys of being naturally endowed. "No fear of popping these babies like the store-bought kind and, if you think for one instance the men folk give two hoots about what y'all think of me, just get a look at Granddaddy's face over there. He probably doesn't even know his own name right now."

That old geezer was staring and drooling. He hadn't heard a word I'd said, but he saw everything. I decided to take one for the team, the team of all the others on the receiving end of the mean girls. I made a pouty face at him. "Mrs. Daniel said y'all need to be going. Come here and let me give you a hug before you leave." He staggered over and, as bad as I hated it, I gave him the full frontal.

The corner of Mrs. Daniel's nose twitched up and she arched her penciled in eyebrow to the point that I thought it was going to crawl to the back of her scalp.

None of us heard Jack's return. "Awe, you have to go so soon? Let me get your purses." His voice was almost triumphant.

The door had barely closed behind the Daniels when Jack turned to me. "No one should ever under estimate you, Caroline Collier."

Chapter 12

"Leave them," Jack referred to the dirty dishes as I headed back toward the kitchen sink. "I'll get them later. Come sit with me."

Jack caught my hand and pulled me along behind him. I followed him up the stairs, around the bend to the hallway and toward the upper deck. Jack stopped at the door and held it open for me. It was then that I realized what had kept him from rescuing me from the Daniel women before he did. There must have been thirty or forty tea light candles dotting the railing of the porch. They twinkled in little glass jars like fireflies.

"It's beautiful," was the only sentence I could form.

Jack took a seat in his usual spot on the chaise, but didn't let go of my hand so I could walk around to mine. Instead of releasing me, he pulled me into his lap. A maneuver or two later and I found myself nestled into him. Propped up against his chest I could feel each breath he took. Each exhale floated down my neck and over my shoulder, blazing a trail of chill bumps. I'd been turned on since I first saw myself in the mirror wearing my new dress and wondering what he would think.

For the first time tonight I was able to relax. I laid my head back on Jack's shoulder and breathed in his cologne. It was that hint of cedar and fabric softener that I'd come to crave. I bent my knees up and crooked my hip so they rested against his right leg. My dress flowed toward the end of the chaise and covered us like a blanket. Only the tips of my toes showed at the end. It was a cool night with a gentle breeze coming off of the water. I was virtually bare up top, but I was warm in Jack's arms.

"I could go to sleep right here just like this," I sighed.

Jack didn't take it as the compliment I meant it to be. "Are you tired? We can call it a night," Jack offered in words that came out in a staccato type rhythm, quick and pointed.

"No, no, that's not what I meant."

"Oh," an air of relief came through with his one tiny expression.

"I only meant that the crashing of the waves, the soft light of the candles and laying here with you like this, if you're trying to put me to sleep..."

Jack let his head rest against mine so when he whispered each word vibrated over my ear. "No, that's not it."

We sat in silence for another few minutes before Jack spoke again. Tracing his index finger from his right hand along the area down from my collar bone where my breasts first started to rise from my chest, Jack whispered to me, "What you said to Leslie and her grandmother tonight was spot on. No man can keep his head about him when you look like this."

His touch ignited me and his words caused my insides to do a victory dance as I gathered my nerve and quietly asked, "Does that include you?"

I squirmed as he traced backward over me following the same path. I felt his head shift and undoubtedly his eyes diverted from my chest. He didn't answer my question, but asked another of his own. "Did you mean to go barefoot tonight?"

I giggled and drew up my feet under my skirt. "I got distracted and forgot to go back for my shoes."

"Distracted, huh?" Jack let out in one chuckle.

"Uh, huh," I gave a bit of a low hum of a response. "Do you like it?"

"I've been wondering all evening what look you were going for; bare feet with this beautiful gown, this hair, these." This time he took a more direct approach. Using that same finger, he traced the straight line where the top met my skin and bound me into the dress. I bulged and arched into his touch.

There was another long stretch of silence between us. I didn't know what to say. There were no words that didn't include begging him to take me. Finally, there was a lead in for the real question that was coming.

"Can I ask you something personal?" Jack began.

"Anything."

"And you won't get upset?"

I began to worry, but assured him he could ask me anything. What could he possibly want to know?

"How many boys have there been for you?"

"Wow! That is personal!" The words popped out without my control.

"I'm sorry. None of my business." I could feel him becoming antsy.

I calmly replied, "There have only been two."

"I hate them." He said it under his breath, but I heard him loud and clear.

I twisted around to face him, sitting with my legs folded under me. I took his hands in mine. "Tell me why."

"Because I can't imagine you with anyone else, but me and I know..." Jack's words faded away. He slipped one of his hands from mine and reached for my face. I closed my eyes and leaned into his touch. He grazed my cheek and ran his fingers down my neck, over my collarbone and down. "With your hair like this and bare to here, you're very swan like."

My breath caught as he hooked a finger behind the material between my cleavage. I opened my eyes to see his locked on mine. My God I burned for him.

"Your makeup is pristine and I can't help but want to ruin it. I've pictured your lipstick smudged all evening."

I straightened my shoulders and leaned over a tad and arched my neck, swan like. "Then ruin it," I panted.

"I want to ruin this dress of yours, too. I want you to blush and think of me when you take it to the dry cleaners."

"Ruin it," I stared at him, never breaking eye contact, as I gathered the flowing material of my skirt with both hands, raised to my knees and stepped over one of his legs and then the other. At the rate we were going I was getting wetter with every word. It was highly likely I would ruin the dress before he did.

"You're going to be the ruin of me," Jack sighed.

"I doubt that, Boss." I braced my hands against his chest and rolled my hips.

"Oh, shit, Caroline! The trouble with you is that you know what you do to me and you know what I want..."

I leaned in deeper to him, any farther over and I would have spilled out. "Stop talking. Ruin my makeup. Ruin my dress. I'm begging you."

One of Jack's hands went under my skirt and started climbing my thigh as the other left my cleavage and took me around my neck. He pulled me to him and devoured my mouth and as he did the hand that was under my skirt found my thong. Having his hand on my bare ass and his tongue slipping in and out of my mouth was mind blowing.

He gripped me and dug his fingertips in, clutching tighter to me, as the hand that was around my neck pulled at the ribbon that tied the back of my dress. It loosened, but I didn't spring free. During all that Jack worked his way from my mouth to my ear to my collarbone. He was headed down and I could hardly wait.

In one fluid movement, Jack caught hold of me and flipped me to my back. "Oh, my God, Jack!"

I wrapped my arms around his neck and pulled him back to me. I wasn't quite in the position he wanted me yet, so he hooked a hand behind my knee and pulled me down in the chaise. I squealed with delight over the shock of him taking control. I loved it!

Once I was where he wanted me, Jack made quick work of the buttons on his shirt. He threw it behind him and it sailed over the balcony railing. I laughed.

"I'll get that later," he said as he refocused on me.

Just having his eyes back on me made me arch and heave toward him. I wanted him desperately, so much more than I'd ever wanted anything or anyone before.

Shirtless, hovering above me, he was perfect. The shape of his arms, his chest, the way he flexed as he leaned down to run his tongue between my tits, that muscular build that only those as lucky as me ever got to see was really something.

"Ruin everything about me," I whispered as I ran my fingers through his hair and he freed me from the top of the dress.

A lick to one nipple and then the other. "Ruin me," I moaned again. I quivered under him.

"I don't think anything could ever ruin you. Not really." Jack looked back at my face and brushed the stray hairs away.

I locked my ankles around his back and pulled him to me. "I love kissing you."

"It hurts to look at you," he breathed. "You are so beautiful."

I pulled his face to mine and rubbed my chest to his as he kissed me. He started with my lips and moved to my neck while rotating a hand around my breast. I was throbbing in a good way.

"I love feeling your skin against mine. That night in the kitchen. You drove me wild. You wanted me to get a good night's sleep, but really the thought of you, the possibility of this, kept me up all night."

"Let me keep you up all night again," I coaxed him lower and again his mouth was all over me.

I could feel it happening, he was hiking my skirt and positioning himself between my legs. I don't know when he dropped trow or how he did it. I knew he didn't take them completely off. They were just down far enough to get free.

There was a moment of hesitation on Jack's part.

"I want you. I need you. Ruin me. Ravage me. Please, Jack."

Hands were everywhere. Mouth everywhere. Thong long gone. My heart raced and my mind spun. All of my senses were alive and awake. Jack was losing that internal fight of his, so I thought. Then he stilled, pulled back, hovering above me and asked some question that no one cared about right then.

"Do you want to go inside? To the bedroom?" He asked.

"No! I want you!" I was breathless and frantic for him to finish what he started.

"Here? Out here?" he clarified.

"Anywhere with you... Now."

My word he took his time about things, but it was so worth it. Jack was some sort of expert when it came to the female body. I pushed away any notions of how he might have gained the expertise that he used precisely on me. It didn't matter. He hadn't lied or over exaggerated his abilities. He hit places in me that I didn't even know existed and left me a shaking, tear stained mess of nerves when he was finished. I'd never screamed before, but he made me scream his name so loud that he covered my mouth for fear that we'd wake Josh.

Jack did what he said he wanted to do. My makeup was smeared. My dress was ruined with my sweat, his sweat and God only knows what all else. I laid there next to him trying to catch my breath, knowing I'd been thoroughly fucked and loving every memory of it. My skin tingled as I listened to him taking in each breath, raggedly, and letting it go the same as me.

Jack rolled to his side, facing me. "How's youth being on your side working out for you?"

I wasn't sure if I could move, but I gathered all the strength I had left, put a challenging tone in my voice and willed my legs to work.

"Blow out the candles and meet me in the shower and you can tell me." I said as I got to my shaky feet.

I tiptoed into the hall and headed toward the door to Jack's room. Until that moment I considered that room off limits. I hadn't even darkened the door once in my time there. After what we'd just done, out under the stars so God and everyone walking along the beach might have witnessed, I figured not much was off limits anymore.

I shimmied out of my dress and left it on the floor in the doorway. It was a giant bread crumb for Jack to find, luring him to me.

The water was starting to steam and fog the shower door real good when I heard the latch come free. I turned to see Jack standing there in all of his naked glory. My mouth watered and I felt flush all over. This was the first time I'd seen him completely nude and he was beyond my imagination. He was hands down the best looking man I'd ever seen. He seemed taller and even at a point where most people, like myself in that same moment, would be at their most vulnerable, Jack oozed confidence.

Shoulders back, chest out, not a thread on him and he didn't make one sound to apologize for his growing arousal. It was the first time he'd seen me naked as well. Until then I'd been somewhat clothed or guarded by shadows, but not now. Heated bulbs in the shower stall lit me from every angle. I had flaws, too many freckles, a few tiny stretch marks on my ass where my hips widened too fast during puberty, and there was no hiding them now. I was as exposed as he was, but unlike him, I was acutely aware of it. I was nervous despite the telltale signs that he liked what he saw.

"I have a feeling I'm going to get a very good night's sleep tonight Miss Collier." Jack entered the shower and took a few steps toward me.

Like the rest of the house, no expense was spared on this bathroom. The entire room was like a spa and the shower alone was bigger than the kitchen in my first college apartment. It was tiled from floor to ceiling in a sandstone color and it was very cave like. There were duel shower heads and more room than the two of us needed, but it was nice. The water was warm, but my body heated from the proximity to Jack.

A few more steps in and Jack pinned me to the back of the wall. The wall should have given me a shocking chill like tile in a shower was prone to do when it touched bare skin, but the heat lamps worked their magic. The only thing that phased me was Jack.

One of my dear friends, the one that I shared the most intimate details of my life once told me that everyone looked better wet and Jack was no exception. One hand held my wrists above my head and the other went with gliding fingers through my damp hair. Despite the water, the waves held as his fingers went through them. His lips were cherry red in this light and he looked like Dracula.

Back against the wall, standing on my toes, Jack gave me a once over. "You are absolutely stunning."

Jack licked his lips and I tried to slip his grasp, but he held me firm. I wanted to wrap myself around him and I wiggled, lusting for him once more. I arched my back from the wall and my breasts stood at attention. Gazing down at them, Jack remarked on their perfection.

Jack grated up me with his chest to mine and both of his hands now locking our fingers and stretching my arms higher. His knee between my legs urged mine to part. Downward he grated over me again and the shock waves in me were building already. Jack bent his knees and this time he was the master of the pelvic hug. There was no material to keep him from me and in one fluid movement, he bucked his hips, straightened his legs and claimed that hollow spot within me.

I gasped from being both penetrated and from the amazement of how he did it. No hands.

My feet were taken from the floor and I was suspended with my weight distributed between the wall and Jack's pelvis. He bucked and grated against me in a tantric rhythm as I kissed him deeply and hard until I was at my brink.

"Oh, my God, Jack, I'm almost there," I warned and he slowed. "No, please don't stop," I begged and writhed under him.

"As much as I want to make you scream again, please don't. If you need to, bite into my shoulder as hard as you like, but no more screaming tonight."

"I'm not going to bite you!"

"You might like it." Jack shoved into me and bit me, right on my shoulder and it was hot. Who knew?

"That's gonna leave a mark," I whimpered.

The tide was rising in me again and I was going to crash soon, but my mind was clear. "I've never screamed before. I don't know what possessed me," I apologized for the second time as Jack steadied the pace, stroking in and out of me.

Locking his eyes with mine, he told me ever so confidently, "I possessed you and I intend to do it again and again and again."

I don't remember at what point he released my arms, but when all was finished and I'd had my second orgasm of the night, I clung to Jack. Pretzel armed around his neck, I kissed him softly near his Adam's apple. "Thank you," I breathed into the kisses.

"For what?" he asked.

"I've never had it twice in one night."

Jack stepped back and looked at me with wonder. "You're kidding."

Suddenly self-conscious, I admitted, "No, not ever."

One question led to another and I was forced into more confessions. "The two..." I began and Jack cut me off.

"Still hate them." Jack reminded me.

"Well, they weren't as talented as you are and, once they got theirs, they were done." I slipped away and started for the shower door.

Jack reached for me and caught me by the wrist. "You won't be having that problem here. Any man that won't satisfy you more than once in a night is a fool," Jack whispered as he took down a towel and wrapped it around me.

It had been about fifteen minutes since he'd last had me, but before I could comprehend what he was implying, he verbalized his intentions, "I'm going to make you come a minimum of five times tonight, Caroline. I'm going to set the bar so high you won't ever forget where I've been. I say what I mean and I do what I say, Caroline."

Chapter 13

We migrated to my room sometime in the predawn hours. The walk downstairs remains a fog and I'm not sure that Jack didn't carry me part of the way. The only thing I knew for sure is that Jack issued orgasms like birthday spankings and I was given one to grown on. Six, I didn't even know that was possible.

When I started to stir around 8:00 a.m. I found Jack right there beside me. Stretching and rubbing my eyes, I wondered what I looked like because he looked fresh faced and bright eyed.

"Have you been awake long?" I tried and failed at not yawning through my words.

"Just long enough to check on Josh and get him sorted out for the morning." Jack pulled me close.

I jumped up in bed. "He doesn't suspect?"

The whole reason we'd moved from Jack's bed to mine was to keep Josh from finding us together.

"No, he's playing in his room and I told him I was helping you clean your room."

I laughed, "Clean my room."

Jack pulled me back and into his arms, kissing me gently. "Are you sore this morning?"

Surprisingly, "No."

"I guess I'll have to try harder." His hands were steadily roaming over me.

"I could get used to waking up like this," I moaned.

"If that's what you want, then we need to move you upstairs," Jack feathered the words over my neck as he rolled me onto my back.

"What?" I sighed.

"We need to move you to the room across the hall from me. We'll let my parents have this room."

For a moment I actually thought he meant he was moving me into his room and that made my stomach flip.

111

I knew that couldn't be it. Jack cautioned me and explained in detail that, although he didn't get around, he never had women spend the night at his house. As many firsts as I was experiencing he was experiencing some, too. This was the first time he'd ever had a woman in his house, in his bed, and the first time he'd allowed one that he was remotely interested in near Josh. He was very protective of his son and didn't want him to become attached.

"Since Josh said he found you first, I don't think there's any way around the attachment issue for him. I think he loved you from the moment he first saw you." Jack explained last night. "Not counting teachers and his former nanny, I think you're the first woman other than my mother that's ever given him more than thirty seconds of their time. I love watching him play with you and seeing his face light up. Caroline, you just don't know what you've done for him."

Jack's parents were supposed to be in around noon so after we "cleaned my room," as Jack put it to Josh, Jack and I got dressed and moved me to the bedroom across the hall from his.

The room I had was fine, but the new room was amazing. It was a mirror image of his with French doors that led to the deck. I could see the ocean from all of the windows and doors from every vantage point in this room. This was the room Jack's parents usually stayed in when they visited, but this time I got their king sized bed and they were downgraded to the queen room. I felt bad putting them out of their room, but Jack reminded me again that it was his house and this was not their room. That didn't make me feel that much better about my chances of endearing myself to them.

"Don't worry about it. My mother will love you." He tried to put my nerves at ease as we remade the bed in the downstairs room.

"And your dad?"

"He loves no one, but himself." Jack threw a pillow case at me. "I know what you're thinking and don't bother seeing it as a challenge to make him like you. Just accept it and ignore him."

"That's kind of hopeless sounding," I frowned. "I want them to like me."

"That's because he's hopeless. Trust me. I know. Plus, I like you. Isn't that enough?"

Having Jack like me was more than enough, but I knew if his parents liked me, that would be like getting bonus points on a final.

Noon arrived and there was no sign of Mr. and Mrs. Belgrave. 1:00 p.m. arrived and as we were finishing lunch they made their grand entrance. They didn't bother knocking, just walked right in.

"Sorry we're late!" Mrs. Belgrave appeared through the entry hall first.

"Grandmommy!" Josh screamed.

Jack and I stood as Josh ran to his grandmother and jumped in her arms nearly taking her down.

Jack's mother stood at what I estimated to be about five foot four inches tall. He clearly hadn't gotten his height from her, but he had gotten her eyes and maybe her hair color. She had bright blue eyes and chestnut brown hair which she obviously had colored. There was no denying she was a woman in her sixties, but that was only a fact I knew due to Jack's age. There was hardly a wrinkle beyond a few crow's feet around her eyes and there wasn't one gray hair on her head as far as I could see from my vantage point.

Mr. Belgrave was a sharp contrast to his wife. He loomed over her by head and shoulders and that was clearly where Jack got his height. He was also a silver fox with his entire head having given way to the grays.

"Josh, please!" Mr. Belgrave demanded and, I knew in that instance, with that sharp tone of voice, to heed Jack's warning about his father. Thirty seconds in the door and the man was already annoyed with Josh, who was only doing what six year olds do, get excited over their grandparents.

I shot Jack a look as we stood from the table to greet his parents.

"See," he said to me.

I smiled and shook my head.

Mr. Belgrave squeezed past Josh and his grandmother revealing the younger woman following behind them. My first thought was that Jack never mentioned a sister. The woman was taller than his mother, but not as tall as Jack and his father. Her features were very sculpted and she was beautiful, but the kind of beautiful that was courtesy of heavy makeup. I remember my father making jokes about women that looked like her.

"You go to bed with Marilyn and wake up with Medusa," he always said.

The hustle and bustle of everyone making their way in and around Josh left me to blend in with the wall. Although I felt invisible, I could see the look on Jack's face change. He reddened and his jaw tightened. He straightened his back and took hard breaths. The tension coming off of Jack was like nothing I'd witnessed from him before. He was less than thrilled to see that he had a third guest.

"Jack," his father beckoned, "We brought Jade with us. She figured there's no time like the present to get started with the new campaign strategies."

Jack wiped his mouth with his napkin and then slung it on the table. "Then she figured wrong."

"Be a good sport and get her bags!" His dad ordered him as if Jack hadn't said a word. His father looked my way, but did little more than raise an eyebrow.

Jack dropped the F-bomb under his breath and gritted his teeth. He reached for me and squeezed my hand. I felt an apology coming, but he didn't give one. "Please run and move your things to my room. Discretely. I'll move them to the other room upstairs later. Go. Please."

Now the color in my own face was draining. The happiness in the house was being sucked out like a vacuum and I hated it. Whomever this woman was, her coming here was not a good thing.

I did like Jack asked. I even hid my suitcases and everything under his bed. I didn't like it, but I did it. This was not an impromptu invitation to stay in his room.

Halfway down the stairs I realized the men were missing including Josh and Jade and Mrs. Belgrave were seated in the living room. Mrs. Belgrave was telling Jade about the indoor camping trip Josh had raved about. I lingered on the steps long enough to realize Jade was not the least bit interested in what Mrs. Belgrave was saying. Her head turned in every direction, but that of Mrs. Belgrave. Mrs. Belgrave kept going. Apparently Josh had called her and gushed over the good time he had thanks to Aunt CC.

Finally Mrs. Belgrave noticed me on the staircase. She stood from the couch. "You must be CC. Josh say's you're Aunt CC."

"Yes, ma'am," I confirmed as I started descending the last few steps.

Jade jumped to her feet as well. "Michael said Jack hired a nanny for the summer." She extended her hand, cutting between Mrs. Belgrave and me.

I'd never heard Jack refer to his father by his first name, but I'd heard Josh's full name, Joshua Michael Belgrave. I assumed the Michael she spoke of was Mr. Belgrave. An assumption I didn't make was that Jade had virtually no manners. Not only did she refer to a man considerably her senior so casually by his first name without any salutation, her body language was deliberately abrasive. She aimed to show me who was in control by stepping in front of Mrs. Belgrave and I didn't like that. It was disrespectful and rude.

I stumbled on the last step, on purpose, and in my attempts to regain my balance I avoided Jade's hand shake altogether. While she sidestepped me, Mrs. Belgrave sprang to my aid, grabbing me to make sure I didn't fall. Jade didn't realize, I was familiar with the games power grabbing women played. I had a sister-in-law that had been training me in those games since I was in my early teen years. I didn't like to participate in such, but it didn't mean I wouldn't. In fact, most of the time, I didn't have to play at all. Most of the time, my personality was such a sharp contrast to women like Jade and Becky that all I had to do was be myself. This was not one of those times. I would have done just about anything to keep from shaking hands with Jade.

"I'm so sorry. I am so clumsy," I apologized to both of them.

While Jade stood with her nose out of sorts, Mrs. Belgrave asked if I was alright. "You've got to be careful on those steps. Jack's such a clean freak, I swear he puts Endust on them. I've nearly busted my own behind on them a time or two."

"Endust?" I laughed. "Is he trying to kill us all?"

Mrs. Belgrave and I bonded instantly. I cut my eyes at Jade thinking, "Now who's the outsider?" I didn't say it out loud, but she knew what was up.

Jade turned on the charm, if one could confuse syrupy sweet cattiness with charm, "Oh, do you need to clean up from lunch? We don't want to keep you from your duties."

"I do need to pick up from lunch. Mrs. Belgrave, would you like to sit at the island and keep me company? Jack tells me you own a chocolate business and he let me try one of your chocolate covered strawberries," I gushed over Jack's mother as she followed me to the kitchen. I grabbed our plates from the table as we went. I sat them by the sink as she began to tell me about the chocolate covered strawberries and other new lines of products they were testing.

I politely stopped her after I'd completely cleared the table. "Would you excuse me for a moment? I need to get Josh." I continued as I washed my hands. "I've been teaching him how to wash dishes and he loves it."

Mrs. Belgrave didn't seem put out or upset when she asked, "You've been doing what?" She sounded impressed.

"I've been teaching him how to wash dishes by hand. It's a pretty basic task, but his wife will thank me one day."

That's when Jade made her contribution to the conversation. "You plan on being around that long. Isn't that kind of presumptuous on your part?"

I shook my head and thought about how I missed Leslie Daniel and her grandmother right then.

"Josh went outside with the men to get our luggage," Mrs. Belgrave informed me.

"Thank you," I said to Mrs. Belgrave, but I didn't say a word to Jade. I figured it was best to act as if I hadn't heard her.

I opened the front door to find Jack and his father in a full blown argument and Josh was nowhere in sight.

"Get her out of here now! I've already said it once. Take her home!" Jack shouted.

"Where are your manners?" His father shouted back. "Get your head out of your ass! She's not going anywhere. She rode with us!"

"How dare you bring someone to my house without clearing it with me first!" Jack puffed out his chest and stepped toward his father. "She's not welcome here and I want her gone! I don't want her in my house!"

"Excuse me," I said just loud enough to get their attention.

Of course Jack acknowledged me, but it wasn't the type of acknowledgement I was used to from him. "Not now, CC."

"Where's Josh?" I asked politely, despite having been snapped at.

"What do you mean? Isn't he in the house with you?" Jack still had his back toward me.

"Shit, Jack! He's not with me!" I glanced around the yard and didn't see Josh anywhere.

I ran back in the house, calling his name and Jack came running after me also screaming for Josh. Mrs. Belgrave realized what was going on and she started calling for him as well. As we raced through the house, the only thing Jade did was stay out of the way.

I ran out onto the downstairs porch facing the water and when Josh wasn't there I continued on to the beach. I ran as fast as my feet would carry me through the sand in my Keds tennis shoes. I stopped about ten yards shy of the water and scanned up and down the beach. People were everywhere. Parents, children, they were on the shore and in the water. The beach was crowded and I must have seen fifteen little boys that looked like Josh from a distance. I screamed his name and Jack came running out to join me.

"Do you see him?" Jack was frantic. We both were.

"I'll head toward the tidal pool," I told him and I kicked off my shoes so I could move faster in the sand.

Jack headed in the opposite direction. I took about ten steps and turned back and called for Jack, "We'll find him," I promised.

"We've got to," he replied and then we both went back to calling for him.

I made it all the way to the tidal pool, checking the face of each little boy and calling Josh's name. I alternated between yelling "Josh" and "Joshua Belgrave".

There wasn't a whole lot beyond the tidal pool at Draper Lake so when I didn't find Josh I turned around and headed back. I scanned every little face in and out of the water on my walk back. I held out hope that Jack had found him or maybe he was hiding in the house somewhere all along and Mrs. Belgrave found him, but there was a queasy feeling in my stomach wondering what if we didn't find him. What if he'd gotten in the water? What if the undertow or a rip current got him? All kind of horrible scenarios played out before my eyes and I was almost in tears when I spotted Jack walking up the beach with Josh in tow. I ran to them and gathered Josh in my arms.

"I love you, Josh, I really mean it so please don't ever run off again because it scares me that I might not ever see you again. It would absolutely break my heart if something bad happened to you." I hugged him as tight as I could without hurting him.

I carried Josh and Jack walked with his arm around me the rest of the way back to the house. Once inside everyone fawned over Josh and how relieved we all were and I blended in like a wallflower again. It gave me the anonymity I needed for a few minutes so I slipped away, ran upstairs, through Jack's bedroom to the toilet room and bawled my eyes out from the relief of finding him. I wasn't his mother, but my heart was sick with panic over not being able to find him for those thirty minutes and the thoughts that something horrible had happened to him was more than my poor nerves could take. I'd had a trying night with the Daniel ladies followed by more joy than I could ever imagine followed by whatever this was with this woman Jade and now all of this. The emotional roller coaster was more than I could handle.

Jack found me sitting on the lid of the toilet crying. "CC, are you alright?"

"I will be. Just give me a moment." I sniffled and wiped my face with toilet paper.

Jack fell to his knees in front of me. "What's wrong?"

"I imagined the worst..." I covered my eyes with my hands. "Where is he now?"

"Josh's fine. He's with my mother. I've had another talk with him about wandering off. He said he thought he saw you on the beach and went after you." Jack balanced with his hands on my knees. "You know, he got upset when he thought you were leaving and now you're upset because you thought he was gone." Jack

119

tilted his head and gave me a little smile. "I'm beginning to think the two of you have something going on."

"It's not funny! Something could have happened to him. We've got to watch him better." I tried to dry my tears, but I wasn't having much luck.

"I know and we will. Maybe he would listen if you gave him the talk about not wandering off instead of me. Perhaps you'll get through to him." Jack paused. "Caroline, where's your makeup case?"

"Oh no, I look terrible." I rolled my eyes and let out a huge sigh. "It's under your bed with the rest of my stuff."

"You look beautiful." Jack squatted on his knees and took my face in his hands and kissed me before he stood up to go get my bag.

"I'm sorry." I said as I followed him as far as the vanity in the bathroom.

"There's nothing to be sorry about." Jack got the case and came right back. "You can't let them see you cry. My mother, fine, but not my father or Jade."

That seemed like the perfect time to ask who she was and why he had the reaction to her that he did. "At first I thought she was your sister or something."

Jack almost laughed as he handed me my makeup. "Definitely not my sister."

"I figured that out pretty fast, but..."

The look on his face said there was an internal struggle within him as to how to explain just who she was. Finally, Jack hopped up on the countertop and started to explain as I touched up my makeup. "You know how sometimes there's a spot on your back that you just can't reach so you need someone else to help you out?"

"What does that have to do with anything?" I asked, stopping with the makeup and looking him straight in the face.

Jack gave a forced smile that begged sympathy. "Jade used to scratch an itch."

120

I understood perfectly what he was saying. My stomach knotted and I no longer wanted to cry. I wanted to slap someone. I wanted to slap her. The look on my face must have given away my every thought.

"You hate her." Jack didn't put it like a question.

My mind leapt back to last night and what he hated. If he thought it was as simple as that, he was sorely underestimating the depth of the emotion stirring in me. Oh, yes, I hated her. I loathed her.

"How a woman like that could ever have gained your affection is beyond me."

"I'm sorry, Caroline. I truly am. I'm going to get rid of her."

"You tried that already and while you got the smack down, Josh wandered off. What was your father thinking bringing her here?"

"Well, he wasn't thinking I had someone else here already."

"How long's it been since..."

"No." Jack stepped closer to me and I backed up.

"Since you met me?" My poor heart was shattering and I was hurt. My hate for her turned to disgust for him. I'm sure it showed on my face as well.

"Caroline, please understand."

"What, that you have specific tastes?" I hissed and let it show in my words. "I suppose she's in the five year range. She's kind of curvy. She was just a place card. I guess that's what I am too, just not specific enough. Did I wear you down or could you not hold out and resist the urge to scratch until she showed up? That's right, campaign manager, she's on the payroll too. Jesus Christ, Boss!"

Face perfect or not, I shoved past him and left the bathroom. Before I could make it to the bedroom door, Jack had a hold of me and jerked me back into his arms. I slapped him and struggled to get away, but he held firm. If I even stung his face he didn't let on.

"Listen to me! You are no one's place card. The itch I have for you, if that's what you want to call it, could never be scratched enough."

Then he kissed me with the force of everything he had from the night before. Resisting him was useless. I couldn't.

When he finally let go of me, I was a melted puddle. I almost started to cry again as he swore he hadn't been with her since two days after he met me.

Chapter 14

When I started back down the stairs, my face appeared as nothing had ever happened. I would have given anything to have stayed upstairs with him, picked up where we left off last night and forgotten this day altogether.

"Sorry about disappearing. On the walk back from finding Josh, Jack reminded me that we needed to make sure the guest rooms were ready. Josh and I've been playing hide and go seek all over the house so another once over wouldn't hurt anything. You'd be surprised where I find Legos and those little green army men." I passed through the living room as I spoke.

I walked right past Mr. Belgrave and Jade and made a point to make eye contact with both of them. I held my head high like they didn't faze me at all, but the truth was if they left now I'd be overjoyed.

Josh was in a chair at the kitchen sink washing the dishes and Mrs. Belgrave was drying them. "Drying is usually my job." I said to Mrs. Belgrave. "Isn't he such a great little helper?"

"He is indeed," she answered.

I threw my arms around Josh and whirled him around from the chair. "If you ever leave this house without an adult again, I am never, ever, ever," I emphasized while I tickled him, "going to make chicken fingers and homemade honey mustard for you again! Do you understand me?"

"Yes!!!" he squealed and giggled.

I carried him over to the kitchen table and sat down in a chair with Josh on my lap. "Seriously," I said to him and I lowered my voice, "I'm not joking now. It would break everyone's heart if something happened to you and when you go out by yourself without an adult something bad could happen to you and I might not ever see you again. And that would make me so sad."

Josh threw his arms around my neck. "I don't want you to be sad."

I felt the waterworks coming again. "I don't want to you to be sad either."

While I spoke with Josh, Mrs. Belgrave and Jack watched from the island area. Both had giant grins on their faces.

Mr. Belgrave walked over first and Jade sauntered over last, sticking a proverbial pin in the balloon that was my moment with Josh. She was nearly as tall as Jack and draped her arms over his shoulders and hung on him.

"It's so awesome that you've finally found good help." Jade's words were just another backhanded compliment in my direction, but I didn't take my eyes off of Josh.

Jack instantly slinked from beneath her and pushed her off of him. "You're the only one here that's on the payroll," Jack told her.

"Excuse me?" his father demanded.

"I hadn't had time to properly introduce you all, but this is mine and Josh's friend Caroline Collier from Atlanta. Most of her friends call her CC. She's staying with us this summer. Josh is friends with her niece, Bailey, and since he does not have any aunts and uncles of his own, Bailey told him that he could call her Aunt CC."

"So you're not the nanny?" Jade spoke up.

"No, she's not. She's a family friend."

"Family friend..." Jade started.

She was likely going to finish the statement with the words, "my ass," but Jack's mother cut her off.

"So, what would you like for us to call you, dear?"

"Caroline or CC, which ever you prefer. My family calls me CC," I replied.

"Well, since you are a member of our family for the summer, CC, it is." Mrs. Belgrave cut her eyes at her husband, giving him a warning look.

"What if your constituents found out a strange young woman was living with you?" His father didn't heed the warning from his mother.

"I for one am not going to be on the evening news broadcasting who I have as a guest in my home. Are you?" Jack questioned his father.

"Well, um, uh..." his father struggled to find a response.

"I don't think it's a good idea," Jade stepped to his father's side in a show of solidarity. "As your campaign..."

Jack snapped her up, "Don't you all think it is a tad bit rude to discuss this with her sitting right here? Have you no manners at all? Please allow me to explain something once and for all. I bought this house, with my money. My name is on the deed and as long as it is, I get to say who comes and goes. Now, if I sell you this house, then you can decide who comes and goes. Until that time, I'd thank you to keep your mouths shut."

Jack then turned his attention back to me. "CC, how do you feel about showing Josh and I Atlanta for the 4th? I'm sure if we left now, we could make it there before dark. Mother, would you like to go with us? Josh, you up for an adventure? We'll take the Jeep and ride with the top down all the way."

Josh was giddy and bounced off of my lap and ran to his grandmother. "Please come with us!"

"Jack, you don't have to do that," I piped up as I noticed the look of shock on his mother's face. He was clearly proving a point, but I didn't think it should be done at her expense.

"No, I want you to feel welcome in my home and I could totally understand if you don't right now. If you want to go home to visit your family and be around people that love and respect one another, then I'll take you." I knew Jack was sincere, but he looked his father square in the face, still making that point.

His father started to speak, but before he could utter a word, Jack shut him down again. "If you have

125

anything other than, 'Nice to meet you, Miss Collier,' to say, then you should keep it to yourself."

Jade acted offended on his father's behalf, even laid a hand over her chest and feigned shock. "Who do you think you're talking to?"

"I'm speaking to my father and I apologize for behaving like this in front of you ladies." Jack reached for his mother's hand and she gave it gladly.

The more I watched the interactions between them the more I got an uneasy feeling about Jade and Jack's father. There was something off there and I couldn't put my finger on it. As I watched them, I thought to myself this would be like my father having a strange bond with Becky. That was such a foreign thought that it was laughable. All of the bickering reminded me of my family, but Jack's father didn't seem to know where his bread was buttered. From the moment they walked in, his allegiance was aligned with Jade. I found that very odd.

"No, no one's going anywhere. Miss Collier, it's nice to meet you. There's no need for you to go home unless you want to. I apologize that this weekend has gotten off to a rocky start. My son has always been very protective of his friends. Unfortunately he seems to have forgotten his old friends." Even when Jack's father was trying to be nice, he was scary.

"On the porch now!" Jack barked at him. "Josh, stay with Grandma."

"Yes, sir," Josh's eyes got wide. Mine and Mrs. Belgrave's did too as Jack grabbed Mr. Belgrave and escorted him to the porch. The only person still unaffected by all of this was Miss Modern.

Mrs. Belgrave asked Josh to show her where we had our campout and the two of them left for the third floor observatory. I began putting away the dishes that Mrs. Belgrave and Josh had stacked by the sink. Jade took a seat in one of the high top chairs at the kitchen island.

"I don't know what's going on with you and Jack, but I don't like it," she sneered.

I ignored her and continued with my task, all along wondering how Jack managed to surround himself with such mean women. First there was Leslie Daniel and her grandmother and now this tart. I didn't think I was anything like them.

"Do you hear me? I don't like it one bit!" She raised her voice. "I don't know what your game is, but it is over."

I wasn't one for yelling or being yelled at so that got my attention. I turned back from the cabinet and slammed the plate that I had in my hand down on the counter with a little more force than I had intended. "Is that so?" I looked her in the eye. My face was completely expressionless.

"I'm here to tell you..." She began, but I didn't let her finish.

"To tell me that he's yours?" I maintained a stone face. "Is this you trying to stake your claim? Let me know that you were here first? I hear you, but woman to woman, let me explain to you, this isn't attractive. If he was yours you wouldn't have to tell me anything."

"Excuse me? I'll have you know Jack and I have been together for years."

"Years? Yep, that's what he said. Well, he kind of said that. Mainly he said something about you being someone to scratch an itch." I wrinkled my nose and communicated through the look on my face that I hated to break it to her.

"Really?"

I shrugged.

"I'm fairly certain that he's not going to need your scratching services for the foreseeable future. By the way," I pointed down the hall. "If you're staying, that's your room over there by the front door. You can put your things in there whenever you get ready."

"Who are you to tell me..."

I motioned to the Louis Vutton luggage set that still sat in the middle of the pass through from the kitchen to the living room. "They aren't going to move themselves and I'd hate for you to fall over them and break your neck."

"Just know, I'll be here to scratch that itch of his long after you're gone."

I told her like my mother used to tell Chris and I about leaving out our toys, "You better get to those suitcases before I do because if I pick them up they're going in the trash."

Jade gave me a look like, "You wouldn't," and I answered out loud, "Yeah, I would."

I didn't know what had come over me. I'd put up with my sister-in-law for so long on account of her being family that since I stood up to her maybe I decided I wasn't rolling over for anyone anymore. I turned the cheek to begin with, but I only had two cheeks so once both had been smacked I came out swinging. No sooner than the door opened and I saw Jack's face, I thought better of having swung for the fence and told Jade about the scratching. I regretted saying that to her, not because she didn't deserve it, but I shouldn't have repeated what Jack told me. It wasn't fair to him. It did do the trick with her. She got out of my face and was moving her own luggage when he came in.

When his mother and Josh returned, Jack asked Mrs. Belgrave to watch Josh for the evening. He told them he'd promised to show me some of the haunts around the up and coming 30A area. His mother was glad to babysit, but his father was none too happy. Despite his best efforts, it appeared Jack still hadn't gotten his point across to his father.

Jack put my things in the room across the hall from Josh's and down the hall from his. He promised me that his father was taking Jade home the following day and that gave me a sense of relief.

Everywhere else we'd been together we'd taken his Jaguar, but this time he pulled the cover off of the Jeep. This was the first time I'd seen what was under the car cover that was in the garage. Top down, a stick shift and Florida Gator orange, it looked like fun and it was.

"Where did you get that dress from last night?" Jack asked as we sat waiting for a car to pass before turning on to Highway 30A.

"A boutique in Seaside." I looked at Jack wondering why he would ask.

Jack gave it the gas and went through the gears as he made a right onto the highway and we headed toward Seaside. He pulled my hand to his mouth and kissed it. "We need to get you another dress."

I giggled, but quickly added, "You don't have to do that."

"I know, but I want to." Jack turned up the radio and I danced in my seat to the sound of Queen's "Crazy Little Thing Called Love." I put on a show for him, lip syncing to the music and keeping time to the beat with facial expressions, shoulders and everything I had.

As we passed the turn for Grayton Beach, Jack asked if I'd ever been to the Red Bar.

"Of course."

"There's not much down here that I can introduce you to, is there?"

"Probably not. I grew up down here, too."

"How do you feel about going shopping and then getting dinner?"

When his right hand wasn't on the gear shift it rested high on my thigh. My leg was bare to my shorts and his touch was exquisite. I would have agreed to anything.

Three stores later, Jack had bought me five new dresses. He insisted I try them all on and come out of the dressing room to model them.

He vetoed six dresses and the ones that he couldn't make up his mind about he bought them anyway. He said it was his money so he got to pick. Two were strapless, one was a halter, one had spaghetti straps and one had capped sleeves. Two were floor length, two were short and the one with the capped sleeves was indecently short.

"Turn around," Jack twirled his finger, giving me instructions. "Let me see the back."

I did as instructed.

"We've got to get out of here before I do indecent things to you in a public place." Jack adjusted his slacks and wiped his brow. Those words concluded the shopping experience.

Shopping wasn't the highlight of the evening. The highlight was dinner. Jack insisted on getting sandwiches to-go from a little deli that was next to one of the boutiques.

As Jack opened the door to the Jeep for me he asked, "Have you ever toured the Wesley house?"

"I've seen the signs, but I've never been." I pulled my seatbelt on as he went around to get in.

"Then you are in for a treat."

There were historic markers along the winding road that led to the state park. I tried to read them, but we passed by them too fast. Soon we parked and Jack carried the sack of sandwiches and canned sodas in one hand and pulled me along with the other. I didn't have to worry about the markers, Jack explained the entire history of the property as we walked.

"The house was built by the Wesley's, a local milling family who owned well over a hundred and sixty acres and ran a saw mill on the property. The Wesley's sold the property and Mrs. Maxon ended up with ten acres and the house. She restored the house to its current grandeur. In 1968 she donated it to the State of Florida and now's it's a state park. Eden Gardens is the name of the park, but the house is still known as the Wesley house. A lot of these live oaks," Jack pointed out, "date back 600 years."

About the time Jack finished giving me the crash course in history the path opened up and I could see the house. White with a porch that wrapped almost all the way around on both the first and second stories, the house was beautiful, but not fitting with the beach scene I was accustomed to around the area. This looked like something that one of us Georgians might find in our own Madison or Washington, some part of our state that Sherman didn't burn.

"They run tours of the house until 5:00 p.m. so they've stopped for the day. I can bring you back another day if you'd like to see inside," Jack offered as we crossed in front of the house.

"I would love to," I admitted, "and I'll bring a camera."

We stood admiring the walkway up to the façade. The red, white and blue of the flag that hung from the second story never looked prettier than against the white background of the house.

"Come on," Jack squeezed my hand and urged me to follow him.

Jack led me along the gravel driveway that aimed toward a water way with a dock that I could see in the distance. We passed by a reflecting pool with a water fountain in it that sat to the side of the house. Every ten paces, I turned and looked back at the house. I couldn't help myself. I wondered if the inside was as pretty as the outside.

Beyond the pool was a live oak that at my best estimation spanned an entire acre. Spanish moss drooped from varying heights, tiny gray ghosts floating up to the branches. Under the branches on the side of the tree closest to the driveway, two ladies were setting up rows of white folding chairs as another lady roped the center aisle off by attaching strands of flowers to the end chairs. They were setting up for a wedding. Jack kept pulling me along until we were walking down the aisle as if the ladies weren't there working.

"No, no," I pulled back. "We shouldn't be here."

"Why? We're not getting in the way." Jack acted as if he might own the place and I started to wonder if he might.

One of the ladies recognized him as we passed her. "Senator Belgrave," she called him.

Jack offered his hand to her. "It looks lovely," he told her and she gushed like she'd met a movie star.

"Are you attending the wedding tonight?" the lady asked.

"No, just giving my friend, Caroline, here a tour of our beautiful state park. You ladies are doing an amazing job. She needs a new venue for her wedding."

"Congratulations," the lady told me as I elbowed Jack in the ribs.

"I'm not really getting married. The senator here is quite the jokester." I made an attempt to correct her assumption, but that just confused her.

"Caroline has always dreamed of a beach wedding, but I think that's only because she's hadn't seen the wedding tree before today."

"There's no prettier place in all of Florida or more magical than right here for a wedding." The lady smiled.

"It's very beautiful," I agreed, "but we shouldn't keep you."

The lady went back to arranging the bouquets along the aisle and Jack took me around to the other side of the tree. He leaned me up against it and it was about five times the width of my back. The trunk of the tree provided a virtual wall between us and the ladies. Jack closed all space between us. He bit his lip and grazed his hand past my cheek and ran his fingers through my hair, cupping the back of my head. I melted into his touch. Even if he wouldn't have said a word, I melted.

"One day, I'm going to get married here. It's going to be a grand affair, nothing like my first wedding, which was little more than an afterthought to the four people who attended it. There'll be aisles of white chairs like this

132

and I'll stand under these branches and watch..." His words broke off.

My heart stopped. Was he about to tell me he would watch me coming? Perhaps he paused because even he knew it was too soon to say such things.

I filled the blank space. "I didn't realize men put thought into these sorts of things."

"Not all of us do, but," he nuzzled into my ear, "sometimes an anomaly comes along and makes us consider things we never thought we would. Sometimes the most unexpected comes along and makes non-dreamers dream."

I shouldn't imagine him waiting under that tree for me, but I did. "I can see Josh standing next to you as your best man."

I could feel his eyelashes bat against my forehead as Jack brought his lips down to mine. Butterflies danced in my stomach at his touch. The kisses didn't stop with his exploration of my mouth. Jack buried his face in my neck and it was all I could do not to breathe the words "I love you" as my toes curled inside of my Keds.

More workers started to arrive and broke up our make out session.

"Feed me and then take me home," I begged.

Jack briefly revisited our current living situation waiting on us at home. "They won't keep me from you tonight."

I bit my lip in anticipation.

Chapter 15

Back at the house we found Jack's mother and Josh in the living room watching an old rerun of the A-Team. Jack's father and Jade were nowhere to be found and that was a relief. Mrs. Belgrave explained that they'd gone for a walk on the beach and that creepy feeling about them returned, but I didn't know what to make of it. I decided whatever was going on there was none of my business.

It was after 8:00 so I offered take Josh to bed. He went willingly and was asleep before I finished reading the first book to him.

After I snuck out of Josh's room as not to wake him I made myself scarce. I went to my new room and settled in for the night. I thought I was waiting up for Jack, replaying his words that nothing would keep him from me tonight, but at some point I fell asleep. I woke up to the sound of a light tapping. Thinking it was on my door I got up, ran my hands through my hair and tried to look alive. I opened the door and didn't find anyone. I stuck my head out and saw Jade in her negligée. She was the one tapping and it was on Jack's door.

I saw the light fall across her as the door opened, but I didn't wait around for him to invite her in or to see him brush her off. My heart broke a little just seeing that witch outside of his door. I sucked it up and tried to trust that he would rebuff her.

I thought of Josh and tiptoed across the hall to get him up and take him to the restroom. When I returned I found Jack waiting in my bed for me.

"I saw Jade..." I started.

And Jack continued, "She's persistent."

"That's putting it nicely." I padded across the floor to the bed and he threw back the covers for me.

"She'll be gone in the morning, I promise," he assured me again.

"It's your house."

"Don't be like that."

"Like what?" I asked as I slipped between the sheets and climbed over to straddle Jack.

"Unfeeling." He steadied me with his hands at my hips. "It's not you."

"And, I get that you're a Gators fan, but this shirt isn't you either." I pinched some of the material of the T-Shirt in my fingers, pulled it up and let it pop back onto his chest. "Being a Georgia girl you can see how this is offensive to my eyes." Although I was joking with him, I kept my face and tone serious.

"Well, I can't have your eyes offended." Jack sat up and the two of us worked together to get the shirt over his head and flung to the floor somewhere by the bed.

For a man of thirty-two, Jack was in impeccable shape. The sight of him with his clothes on made my mouth water. Seeing him with his shirt off, made me wet in other places. Even though I didn't like her, I could understand why Jade wasn't so eager to give up on him.

Tonight Jack was tender and he took his time. From the way he looked at me to the way he slid his hands over me as he undressed me, every act drew me closer to him. I didn't have to ask for anything and I didn't want for a thing. Tonight I didn't feel ravaged. I felt cherished. I felt loved.

"I don't mean to be a lightweight, but six isn't necessary unless you, umm?" I confessed. I didn't want to have to spell it out for him. I adored every single moment of love making or sex or whatever was going on with us, but I was mentally, emotionally and physically spent.

Jack shifted me to cradle my head against his chest. I could feel his heart still racing. "One, six, however many you want Caroline."

"I want infinity and beyond with you, but maybe we should pace ourselves."

135

"Infinity, huh?"

I rolled over to face him and scooted up so I could reach his face. I placed a chased kiss on his lips. "And more."

"I like the sound of that."

"You do?" Every now and then I needed reassurance. I couldn't help it.

"More than you know." Jack licked his lips and got that far away look like he was searching the depths of his mind for something.

"Did you ever read 'A Tale of Two Cities' when you were in school?" I propped up on my elbows so I could see his face better.

"Yeah," Jack was back to the present and clearly curious as to why I would ask about such.

"Today has been like the opening lines from that book, 'It was the best of times and it was the worst of times.' Today was awful and wonderful at the same time. I think it goes without saying, this is not what I expected when it came to meeting your parents. Granted, you warned me about your father, but Jesus, who knew? And, Jade." I rolled a heavy breath out and carried on. "It's one thing for me to tell you I've had two lovers, it would be quite another for one to show up."

Jack interrupted me, "It's not always going to be like this."

I placed my index finger to his lips. "Shh. Let me finish," I said quietly, "My point is this: I'd endure all of it again for that moment with you under the wedding tree. I appreciate the shopping spree, but you really know how to make me melt for you and shopping isn't it."

Jack flipped me to my back and brought his face down to mine. "What am I going to do with you? You are so unbelievable. Gorgeous, smart and here with me."

"You know you're going to break my heart," I sighed.

"You only say that because you don't know the power you have over me. I'd break all the rules for you."

Jack planted a quick kiss on my lips and then got up from the bed. "Come on, I'm not sleeping like a guest in my own house and you aren't either. I want you in my bed."

"What about Josh?"

Jack tossed me the Gator shirt. "Put this on," he told me as he got his pajama pants up.

"You know I'm a UGA grad." I slipped the shirt on. "Seriously, what about Josh?"

"We'll lock the door. Caroline, this is a first for me, but we'll figure it out."

"Okay." I got a look at myself in the mirror wearing the Florida Gator shirt as we started for the door. "You know my diploma is on fire and my parents' house is probably burning down right now."

"And you make me laugh."

I grabbed my night shorts and slipped them on before heading down the hall behind him. Through the doors at the end of the hall, I could see one of the candles from last night flickering again. It was after 11:30 p.m. and I thought everyone had turned in for the night, but someone was out there.

"Jack," I whispered, "Someone's on the porch."

Jack gave a tilt of his head and tried to make out who it was. "It's just my mom."

"Let's go sit with her for a little while?" I suggested.

Jack looked me over. "Are you sure? I wouldn't want that shirt to burn through your skin. I know how you Georgia people are. That's probably like sunlight on a vampire to you. Psssss." He made a stinging sound.

"I'm not afraid if you aren't," I stepped ahead of him, closer to the door leading to the porch.

"What would I be afraid of?" he asked.

"Having to explain to your mother why I'm wearing your shirt at this time of night and why we're sneaking around your house," I challenged him.

"You assume I haven't told her all about you already?"

137

My face turned a thousand shades of red. "What did you say?"

"Now who's scared?" Jack taunted me.

"What must she think of me?" I sighed.

"Why do you care so much what she thinks?"

My eyes widened as if he was daft for asking such a question. "Because she's your mother."

"So you want my mother's approval?"

"You are exasperating! Are we going out there or not?"

Jack held the door and as I stepped through I received a smarting smack on my ass. When I yelped from the sting his mother snapped her head around to see us.

"Sorry," I bit my lip and tried to hide my smile. "Do you mind if we join you?"

"Not at all." Mrs. Belgrave was in the double chase where Jack and I usually sat, where he'd ruined my dress just the night before and where I couldn't look without fear of blushing.

"I thought you'd gone to bed," Jack told her as he pulled the Adirondack chairs closer to her for us to sit in. He offered me the chair closest to his mother.

"I'm real sorry about your father," Mrs. Belgrave apologized to both of us.

"It's par for the course, Mom."

Before Jack and his mother sank into some sort of depression or walk down memory lane over his father, I seized the moment to change the subject. "You know what I've been wondering? I've been wondering what is it like to be a senator. I mean, I've never even been to Washington, D.C. We have a replica of the White House in Atlanta."

Their eyes were trained on me.

"Seriously, it's off of Briarcliff Road and it's an exact, to scale, replica with the exception of the wings. I've driven by it a number of times, but that's the closest I've come. So, what's it like?"

138

"I don't think anyone's ever asked me that before." Jack leaned back in his chair and I could see the wheels in his head start turning.

I continued, "I went to a Bon Jovi concert with one of my cousins last year. We had seats so close that I could see the veins in his neck when he belted out the lyrics to 'Wanted.' Every time he moved, even a twitch, the women went wild. Not that I want women going wild over me, I wondered what that was like."

"I assure you being a Senator is nothing like being Jon Bon Jovi," Jack laughed.

"So what's it like? Tell us Jack," his mother joined in.

"Alright, I'm no celebrity for one, but the best part of being one is being able to be on the floor of the actual Senate. The first time I crossed the threshold of the room, it was as if I was somewhere I wasn't supposed to be. I know, my father was there before me and I'd been elected, but still, it was like I was trespassing, like I was breaking and entering or something. Two years in and I still feel that way sometimes."

Mrs. Belgrave and I leaned in so we could hear him better and over the sound of the tide.

Jack went on, "There's so much history there. Can you imagine being basically in the spot where a hundred men and women have gone before you. They've voted and argued on the merits and opposition of slavery. I could show you the exact spot where Senator Preston Brooks of South Carolina caned Senator Charles Sumner of Massachusetts in 1861. It led to the death of the senator from Massachusetts two days later and fueled the fire that helped start the Civil War. And that's not all."

The passion with which Jack spoke was riveting. I was seeing a whole other side to him and it drew me to him more.

"There's hardly a day that goes by when I'm there that I don't feel the ghosts around me. The tension that lingers in the room, not from the decisions we're making now, but it's the place where our forefathers voted to chase the American Indians from their land, where they voted to send boys and men to their deaths in the world wars and it's where fourteen men paid their dues before becoming president."

"Yeah, there's some decisions made for personal gain, some for political gain, for power, for money, but most of it really is done with the best of intentions and the best interest of our country at heart. It's foremost in arenas where our history is made and I am in awe of it. Every minute that I'm there is a gift."

Mrs. Belgrave took a sip of her wine and then offered Jack her glass. "In all the years your father served, I never heard him speak of it like that. I never thought to ask him what it was like because it just seemed like so much was classified."

Jack took a swig. "It's not all like that. There's some stuff that's classified. I mean, I'm just a junior senator right now so there's a lot that I'm not involved in. I'm considered idealistic so the lifers don't trust me yet."

Jack laughed again and dropped his head back on his chair. "It's funny, my platform for getting elected was 'Change' and yet the very reason I got elected was because of my name. I'm not saying voters are stupid, but they saw the name Jackson Belgrave, ignored the 'Jr.' on the end, and clicked the box. I was elected because I was the same old familiar Republican name on the ballot."

"I don't care how you got there. I'm proud of you." His mother reached over and patted his leg. "I'm also sleepy so I'm going to call it a night. And, Caroline?"

"Yes, ma'am?" I answered.

"My son's a good man and he seems to think the world of you. Try not to break his heart, alright?" Mrs. Belgrave gathered her wine bottle and glass.

Jack took my hand as I responded to his mother. "I think I'm the one who's going to be heartbroken."

As soon as Mrs. Belgrave went inside Jack thanked me.

I didn't understand. "For what?"

"For being you." Jack guided me into his lap. "For making me think about my future again and think that I might be able to play some part in how it shapes up."

"You say that like you were some bystander watching your life go by. You have such a great life that I find it hard to believe you weren't an active part in it."

"I have advisors, my father, Jade, there are others."

"And you always do what others tell you?"

"Not anymore."

Chapter 16

In all of the turmoil that had been my life in Georgia over the last six months nothing prepared me for what was coming. In all of my dealings with Becky, nothing prepared me. Through my sister-in-law's constant cattiness, the end of an era with my college graduation, the loss of my father's company and the financial ruin of my parents, I never expected a summer fling. I never expected to fall in love and I certainly never expected the highs and lows that came with Jack especially not the lows that were brought on by the people in his life.

As the sun rose over the Gulf of Mexico it blared into the bedroom that I'd shared with Jack, his bedroom. It was a grand room that faced the beach and the centerpiece of the room wasn't the massive, fluffy, king sized bed, it was the man that lay sprawled out in it. He was the eighth wonder of the world to me. He was my pillow, my protector, my friend and now my lover. Just looking at him, watching him sleep, took my breath away. He was every star in my sky and the moon and the sun too. As long as yesterday had been, the weeks with him had ticked by like minutes. I didn't know how I was going to leave him and return to school.

I was awake for thirty minutes or more just lying there with my head on Jack's chest listening to his heart beat. I hoped it beat for me the way mine did for him. It had only been just over a month since I'd met him, but I knew, in fact, I'd known for a while, that I loved him. It was so fast, but I knew.

I looked up at him and ran my finger over his Adam's apple. Jack twitched ever so slightly and rolled his head from one side of his pillow to the other. He was beautiful. I kissed my finger and took it from my lips to his. It crossed my mind to wake him, make love to him and set the tone for the day. I didn't. It took great restraint, but I resisted the urge.

142

I slipped from the covers and, as quietly as I could, I went back to the room down the hall where my suitcases had been moved for the third time yesterday. I ditched the Florida Gators shirt, hiding it in the bottom of my suitcase with the button up shirt he'd given me from the night of the hugging incident. I dressed quickly and headed down stairs to the kitchen.

The smell of bacon woke half of the occupants of the house. I could hear footsteps coming through the ceiling above me as I was making breakfast. The room directly above the kitchen was the bathroom that went with the room Jack's parents were staying in.

Jack's father was the first to venture downstairs. He was dressed for the beach and in no way did he appear to have any plans to drive Jade back to wherever it was she came. He was even shirtless, which my father would have never been at this time of morning especially with people in the house other than direct family members. Modesty was not wasted on Jack's father.

Mr. Belgrave took a seat at the kitchen island. He didn't even bother speaking to me as I forked the pieces of bacon from the frying pan and onto the platter with the others that were already done. He helped himself to a slice straight from the platter to his mouth.

"Quality check," he said as he chewed. No good morning.

My brother sometimes said and did similar things when I cooked. I could always tell Chris was joking with me, but this, the way Mr. Belgrave said it, it didn't seem like he was joking with me. It seemed like another comment tossed into the air with no care from him as to how I might take it.

I didn't respond. I turned back around to the stove and added more bacon to the frying pan. I hoped he'd get his sample of the bacon and move on, but he didn't. The pan was full and I had to move on to mixing the batter for the French toast or that wouldn't get done. Thinking I wouldn't be intimidated by him, I turned back

143

around and went back to my side of the island. I'd already put out all of the ingredients so I focused on adding them to the bowl.

"So how long are you staying?" Mr. Belgrave asked me while he chomped on his third or so piece of bacon.

I hadn't thought much about leaving and doing so then made me a little sad. That's probably what he wanted.

I suppose I took longer than he wanted for me to answer. "So, not speaking this morning?"

"No." I furrowed my brow, spoke softly and beat the eggs a little harder. "I'm staying until the second week of August."

"Speak up. I'm not going to bite... unless you want me too." From my chest he made his way back up to my eyes as the words slithered out of his mouth.

I had my fair share of dealings with lecherous men and their comments rarely shocked me, but this was a first. It was both shocking and offensive coming from who I considered to be my boyfriend's father.

Without a word, I cut the stove off and made my way around the opposite end of the island with the intention of leaving the kitchen. I don't know why I bothered choosing the far end, either way I would have to go by him to get to the staircase to go back up and hide. This was the utmost of uncomfortable. This beat yesterday in spades. I wanted away from him. I wanted to run back upstairs to Jack.

I didn't get far. Mr. Belgrave hopped off of the chair where he'd been perched and darted my way. He was quicker than I expected for a man his age and he met me at the corner before I could switch gears and start back around the other way.

"Please let me pass," I said, still trying to maintain an element of politeness and respect.

"Oh come on now. I just want to see what all the fuss is about." He didn't budge except when I backed up

144

to go around the island the other direction. He closed in on me. "I mean, it's not like my son hasn't had other pretty women."

I backed up quicker and he lunged at me, grabbing me by my wrist. His grip was so tight that I couldn't jerk away or make a fist.

"Let go of me!" I was starting to panic, but I wasn't fully there yet so I didn't scream. "You're going to leave a mark!" I said as I twisted, still trying to get free of him.

"Isn't that what you young girls like these days? What's the saying, 'If it isn't rough it isn't fun?'" A swift tug and he snatched me up against him and pinned me between him and the stove.

I was in a full blown panic then. Where was Jack? I wanted to scream. I warned Mr. Belgrave that I would and I continued to struggle. I shoved at him and pushed with all I had.

"I bet you're a real cat in the sack!" he taunted me.

He tried to kiss me and I went for a knee to his groin, but he blocked me. He was every bit as tall as Jack, but wiry. He wasn't toned, but his strength out matched mine. I caught a glimpse of the frying pan in my peripheral vision. I went limp and when he relaxed his grip on me and came in to try to kiss me again, whispering, "That's a good girl," I got a hand free and on the handle of the frying pan. In a haze of fright I swung. The pan went flying, hot grease and all. It got me. It got him. It got him worse than it got me, so I thought. The pan hit the floor with a thud, but who could hear it for all of Jack's father's screaming.

"Goddammit!" Mr. Belgrave screamed in writhing pain, doing a dance and wiping at his chest.

Pumped full of adrenaline from fighting him off, I didn't feel a thing. "Don't you ever put your hands on me again!" I was just about to finish that sentence with "or I'll kill you!" when everyone else in the house came running.

Mr. Belgrave, still jumping from one foot to the other was the first to assure them everything was alright. "CC was turning around with the frying pan when I snuck up on her. I'm so sorry, dear. I didn't mean to scare you."

He was such a liar.

"Oh my God, Michael," Jade shoved past me and I started backing up out of the way. "That's going to blister!"

Jade hardly let Mrs. Belgrave near him.

"Caroline, are you alright?" Jack asked me.

I'd backed all the way to the refrigerator and braced myself against it. I didn't really hear Jack. My mind was going a million miles a minute, first stuck then spinning and then stuck again. Had his father really planned on raping me right there in the kitchen with everyone in the house? As much as I knew what had happened just then, I couldn't wrap my mind around it. I was clearly Jack's girl so why would his father do that to me? Try that?

"Caroline!" Jack said my name a little louder. "Dear Lord, your arm! Let me get some ice."

Jade was busy trying to get to the ice machine on the door of the refrigerator as well. I just stood there.

"Move!" she shouted at me, my ears heard her through the back end of a megaphone.

"Mama," Jack called, "I think she's in shock. Look at her arm."

Apparently my arm was burned. I didn't feel it. I continued backing up, backing up, out of the way of Jade.

Mrs. Belgrave, I could see her, but it was like looking across a football field. She was close, but I was far away. When she saw me, her mouth fell open.

"Jack, don't touch her!" She dropped what she was doing with her husband and started my way. "Caroline, sweetie, we need to get you to a hospital. Jack, get the car."

"Caroline, it's going to be okay. Jade, stay with Joshua," Jack yelled as he darted out of sight.

146

Mr. Belgrave got to his feet. "Barbara, how bad is it?"

Barbara, that must have been Mrs. Belgrave's first name. She shot him a look and he looked at me. His eyes blew up like balloons that were going to burst in his head. I looked down at my arm. What I saw looked like the strips of half fried bacon had landed from my wrist to my elbow on my inner arm. I wiped at it and was immediately brought back to the present.

The pain was blinding and I screamed like the souls burning in the bowels of Hell. My knees went weak and I was on the verge of passing out when Mr. Belgrave caught me. He picked me up and carried me out to the car. I was too weak to fight.

"I'm so sorry, CC. I never meant... I'm so sorry. I'm not going to hurt you." I think he might have been sincere, but I was so out of it trying to breathe through the pain.

Jade ran out behind us. "Give her this," she said, handing Mrs. Belgrave the bottle of Evan Williams that Jack kept in the liquor cabinet. "It will numb the pain a little until they can give her something."

Mrs. Belgrave helped me turn up the bottle and I drank until my throat burned, but it didn't compare to my arm. From the look of it, the scalding grease flew past his chest and the bulk of it landed on my arm. I'd fried an entire pound of bacon by the time the incident happened so the pan was full.

Jack stayed by my side the entire time at the hospital. He held a cool cloth to my forehead and stroked my hair as I laid there. Between the liquor they gave me and whatever was in the IV, I was in and out of it.

I remember begging Jack not to leave me, but that was about it.

I heard some whispering. "It's the worst burn of that kind I've ever seen," said one of the nurses.

I couldn't see Jack among those fussing over me.

"Jesus, it looks like raw meat," said another.

They wheeled me into another room and I opened my eyes. There I found Jack, head in his hands, waiting on me. He immediately got up and darted to the side of my bed.

I looked up at him and through my drunken, drugged stupor, I remember saying to him, "You're so good looking." I sighed, "I love you." I think I passed out again after that.

I woke up back at Jack's house, in his bed. I assessed the room. Jack was propped up in a chair across the room. I looked at my arm laid out next to me. I had a bandage from my fingers to my elbow on my right arm. I could feel a hundred bee stings where my skin used to be.

"Jack." I squeaked out his name, but he didn't budge.

I cleared my throat and said his name a bit louder. "Jack."

He leapt to his feet and was instantly at my side. "What do you need? I'll do anything. Are you in pain?"

"Did you call my mother?" My throat was scratchy.

"No. I didn't know what to tell her. What happened this morning?"

I clammed up. I didn't want to talk about that. Tears sprang to my eyes and I wiped them away with my left hand. "Please call my mother."

"Do you want to go home, Caroline? I'll take you if you want to go? I'll fly with you if you like." Jack sounded defeated.

"No, do you want me to go? What did your father say happened?"

Jack eased into the bed next to me. "I don't want you to go. I'll call your mother for you and, even though I don't want to, I will take you home if you want. I'm so sorry this happened to you. I'd take the pain away from you if I could."

I started to cry and Jack wiped my eyes before gathering me in his arms. "Tell me what happened."

148

"I don't want to," I sobbed. "I just want things to go back to the way they were."

Jack held me as I cried.

"Tell me what really happened," Jack pleaded.

"You won't believe me," I sniffled as I held him as tight as I could with my arm like that.

"Why would you say that?" He leaned back and looked at me. "You're even beautiful when you cry." Jack shook his head. "Of course I'll believe you."

The problem was I didn't believe what had happened, but I started to tell Jack. "I feel so stupid. Your father scared me so bad. I mean, I guess he meant to just scare me. He came on to me. Heavily. I'm not sure what I thought he was going to do, but he frightened me so bad that I fought him off."

"You fought him off?" Jack was puzzled.

"I'm sorry," I started to cry again. "All of you were in the house so surely he wasn't going to... I guess... I mean, well, I don't know him and he was so...hostile... I thought he was going to..." I couldn't bring myself to say it.

"Caroline. Caroline. Caroline. It's okay. You're safe now. I'm with you."

"You don't believe me, do you?" I couldn't stop crying.

"Unfortunately, I do believe you. I don't think he would have raped you. I mean, there've been rumors for years..."

"Rumors?!" I tried to sit up in the bed.

"Why he was forced out of the Senate. He gets a little forceful with the ladies. Lay back down. You don't need to exert yourself."

"Exert myself? We're so far past me exerting myself." I held up my very bandaged arm for Jack to get a good look at.

"I know and I can't tell you how sorry I am about that. I really think he was probably just trying to scare you off. I'm so sorry Caroline. I don't know if it matters, but they're gone." I continued to sit up in the bed and face Jack. I was starting to remember more of what I heard when they thought I was out of it at the hospital. I heard a very heated discussion between Jack and Jade. "You threw them out?"

"I did. Well, I threw my father and Jade out."

"For me?"

"For you and for my mother." Jack hung his head. "I told my mother she could stay, but she offered me some time alone with you and I took her up on it. She took Josh home. I hope you don't mind."

"I don't mind, but what do you mean she took him home?" My gut wrenched and in an instant I missed Josh. "You didn't have to send Josh away on my account."

"I thought you might like a little time to recuperate. Anyway, it's only for a few days and she took him home to my house, where we live when we're not here." Jack reminded me that this wasn't their permanent home.

"Your father and Jade are an item, aren't they?" I asked him.

"You're very perceptive."

"Did your mother know before today and does she know the real reason I got burned?" My heart ached for his mother. I couldn't imagine what my mother would be like if she suddenly found out my father was having an affair or trying to have multiple affairs. She would be devastated.

"She suspected." Jack paused. "Who am I kidding, she's known for years. About the affairs, I mean, but not that he basically forced himself on women. Just to be clear, I don't think he's ever raped anyone."

"You're so calm about this." I cocked my head, glaring at him, trying to comprehend.

"I'm calm now, but you were sedated for most of the day so you didn't see everything that went on. I'm calm now because I already told you that you don't need to exert yourself."

Jack carefully pulled me into his arms. "I don't know what I would do if something happened to you. I'm going to tell you again, if you want to go home, I understand. I won't force you to stay. I'll take you whenever you're ready if that's what you want."

"I don't want to go home unless you want me to go."

Jack gently lifted my face to his and locked his eyes with mine. "I don't want you to go. I know it's just a burn, it's not like you nearly died today, but I really thought I'd lost you. I thought you'd want to run as fast as you could as soon as you could."

I shook my head no. "I want to stay with you. It's going to take more than a lecherous old man and some bacon grease to scare me off."

Jack laughed.

"Jack, did I say anything while..."

"We'll talk about that later." Jack ran his fingers through my hair. "Let's just say you are very beautiful and very amorous when you are drunk and high on pain killers."

After a few minutes, Jack leaned over and got the phone. I told him my parents' number and he dialed.

Chapter 17

July 4, 1997...

"I can't believe I am missing summer in Atlanta. My mother said the whole city is about to stand on its head. It hasn't rained in days and there's talk of cancelling the big fireworks shows for fear of fire hazards," I explained to Jack over breakfast, breakfast that we didn't eat in the kitchen of his house that morning.

"What did your mother say when you told her about your arm?" Jack asked as he perused the menu at The Doughnut Hole. He was treating me to breakfast at his favorite restaurant in all of Florida.

Jack hadn't heard the conversation last night. Most of the time while I was on the phone, Jack spent moving all of my things into his room. That was a detail I didn't bother to tell my mother while I was on the phone with her.

"She insisted on coming to get me, but I convinced her that wasn't necessary." I laid my menu down on the table. "What's your favorite thing here?"

"My favorite thing is the cheeseburger, but since we're here for breakfast, probably the Key Lime doughnut. They're famous for it."

"Okay, Key Lime it is."

The server came and Jack gave her our order.

"Thanks, Senator Belgrave," the girl was flirty in her tone. She might as well have said, "Come hither."

Jack responded with an embarrassed smile.

"Another fan," I picked at him, "Senator Belgrave," repeating the girl in a sultry voice as I ran my foot up his leg under the table.

Jack leaned over the table closer to me. "How's your arm feeling?"

"Fine. It tingles a little, but the pain meds are pretty effective."

"Good," he came even closer, "because if you call me Senator Belgrave like that again I'm going to take you home and make you scream it."

I met him in the middle of the table, my lips almost to his, "Senator Belgrave."

"What am I going to do with you?"

"Make me scream." I bit my lip and slid back into my chair.

"Has anyone ever made you scream before?" Jack kept his voice quiet to make sure other patrons in the restaurant didn't hear him, but I definitely heard.

"Why do you ask questions like that?" I didn't want to know about his activities with other women. Even though I knew they did, I wanted to pretend they didn't exist. I didn't understand why he asked such things.

"Because I want to be the only one that can do that to you."

"You are. You're the only one." I don't know what came over me, but I felt tears rising in my eyes.

"What's wrong?" Jack noticed.

I dabbed my eyes and pushed away the water works as I confessed, "I don't want you to ask me about the others anymore. I wish you were the only one for all of it and I'm sorry that you're not." It was the strange feeling of guilt as if I'd given away something of his.

"Caroline, please," Jack reached across the table to take my hand, but I pulled back.

Jack withdrew and I noticed him running his thumb over his knuckles on his other hand as he figured out that he probably shouldn't ask such things. "You're right. I shouldn't ask you things like that." Jack was silent for a moment before he confessed. "I hate the thought of anyone else touching you."

I hadn't noticed until then that the knuckles on his right hand were busted.

"What happened there?" I nodded toward his hand.

"Don't worry about it. It's nothing." Jack slid his hands into his lap where I couldn't see them anymore.

"It didn't look like nothing."

"We all have our battle wounds from yesterday. Can we leave it at that?"

I really wanted more details. Very selfishly, I wanted to know he'd punched his father's lights out over me, but I didn't press him.

The waitress brought our drinks. Jack and I thanked her. I looked at her when I spoke, but he never took his eyes off of me.

"What am I going to do when you leave?" We still had a little over a month together, but it sounded like he was as weighted by my eventual departure as I was.

I twirled my straw around in my orange juice, picking at the pulp. "I don't want to think about that yet." I opted for changing the subject. "What do you have planned for the rest of the day? What would you like to do?" I took a sip of the juice and batted my eyes at him as I did.

"What do you feel like doing?" A question with a question.

"You." I let the word hang in the air between us before I replied with a more appropriate answer. "You said you'd take me on a tour of the Wesley House. Could we do that? We could go back to the house and I could make us a picnic lunch. We could put out a blanket under that tree or not. I wouldn't want to taint that place for you."

"Taint it? What do you mean?" His look was as questioning as his words.

I looked around to make sure no one could see before slipping my foot out of my flip flop and running my toes up Jack's leg to his inner thigh. "We don't want you thinking of me while your future bride is walking down the aisle."

Jack's eyes heated and he slid down in the booth, giving way to my touch. "I'm willing to take my chances."

154

When the waitress returned with our doughnuts, Jack placed a to-go order for two boxed lunches. After she left, he explained to me once more that I wasn't allowed to exert myself. "Except in certain circumstances," he gave me a wink.

The rest of breakfast Jack and I discussed Josh. Jack called him last night and he called him this morning.

"I love the way you are with him." I know I had that weepy adoring look on my face when I looked at him. Most of the time I saved looking at him like that when he wasn't looking, but I couldn't help myself when he spoke of Josh.

"He asked how you were," Jack said in between bites. "My mother said you're all he talks about."

"My mother probably says you and Josh are all I talk about," I grinned. "Seriously, did you tell him I was fine except for missing him? I really hate that..."

"Caroline, don't worry about it. He's having a great time and my mother needs the distraction now."

I picked at my food. "I wish things were back the way they were three days ago. I hate that all of this happened because of..."

Jack had a way of finishing my sentences. "Oh, please don't say because of you. With the exception of you getting hurt this stuff with my father was long overdue." Jack was adamant.

"Still, I hate it." I took another bite and was fine with closing that subject.

"Don't get me wrong, I miss Josh, but I can't say that I'm not happy to have you all to myself for a few days. There's nothing quite like competing with a six year old."

I blushed and hid my face in my hands.

Later, after the tour of the Wesley House, we spread a blanket out under the wedding tree on the far side from the house. The trunk of the tree was so wide that it shielded the view of us from the house. Jack laid back on the blanket and offered me his chest to lay my head, but I didn't accept. I laid down parallel to him, on my side. Jack rolled to his side to face me.

"You have the prettiest eyes of any man I've ever seen," I said as I ran my hand softly over his face. The stubble prickled at my fingers. Jack cocked his head into my touch. I wondered if it felt like lightening popping against his skin when I touched him like it did for me, but I didn't ask.

"I don't think anyone's ever told me my eyes were pretty before." I continued dragging my fingers down his chin to his neck and he arched as I went. "If you keep this up..."

"You'll never be able to think of anyone but me when you're here?" I scooted closer to him. "Good."

Jack draped his arm over me and pulled me to him. He nuzzled into my neck as his hands started to wander. "Can you see the house?"

I looked, but all I could see was the trunk of the tree. "No." My heart rate was picking up.

"Tell me if you want me to stop," Jack rolled me to my back and slipped his hand under the skirt of my sun dress and slowly came up my leg. "My God, you're so smooth," he aired his observation before planting his lips to mine.

"It's broad daylight," I panted when he raised up from me, focusing more on my panties.

"Do you want me to stop?" His hand continued to climb and he kissed me again.

I couldn't think straight and all inhibitions were disappearing. "No."

"Good. I want to hear you scream my name here."

Remembering my surroundings, I squirmed. "We can't do this here." I was beaded with sweat and resisting him was torture, but we just couldn't.

Jack's arms and body went limp around me. "You're cruel." He took a hard breath and rolled over to his back.

156

"You're a Senator with a reputation to protect. Someone might catch us and you don't really want tourists getting photos of..."

"Of course. Of course. You're right."

"Dignity and self-respect, Senator Belgrave," I taunted him as I straightened out my dress and underpants.

"Potato, pototo. Pish, posh." He pulled me onto his chest and kissed me feverishly.

When Jack let go of me, I was almost ready to rethink my position of self-respect and restraint, but I didn't. "You really are quite bent on ruining this place for yourself, aren't you?" I teased.

"I'll never be able to look at this tree again without getting a hard-on just thinking about you, but I wouldn't necessarily call that ruined." That twinkle in his eye was shining at me.

I covered my face and laughed. "I've never had anyone talk to me the way you do."

"How's that?"

I was embarrassed to say and turned my face away. "No one's ever told me about *that* before."

"What? That they get hard over the thought of you?" Jack wasn't playing anymore. He was quite serious.

"Or that they were going to ruin my dress."

"Does that bother you? That I tell you what you do to me and what I'd like to do to you?"

Despite my embarrassment in talking to him about it now, I replied honestly. "No."

"So no one's ever told you, said stuff to you before, but you like it?"

"When you do it."

I waited a minute before asking, "Do you talk to everyone like this?"

Jack responded in a snap. "God, no!"

"Have you ever brought anyone else here?" I turned back over on my side to face him.

157

A few strands of my hair fell across my face and Jack was quick to tuck them behind my ear and, as he did, he told me, "Not like this."

I felt the wind leave my sails. "But there's been someone."

Jack glanced toward the dock that went out into the water. "I bring Josh here and we fish in the Tucker Bayou."

I was so relieved that it must have shown on my face.

"So, no," Jack added, "I've never brought another woman here and I've certainly never done this here." Jack placed his hand on my thigh and inched up my dress again.

"What am I going to do with you?" I cooed over his touch.

"I have some ideas." He slid his hand higher and I giggled.

"Senator Belgrave, you are just plain naughty."

Jack and I wiled away the afternoon under the wedding tree. He told me about all of his parents' plans for him and how he always worked hard to please them. He assured me he wasn't complaining because he had Josh and they had a pretty comfortable life, but he often felt like everything was mapped out for him and sometimes he had no real say in his own life. He said it was evidenced by his first marriage.

"We were a terrible match and I don't want to sound like I feel lucky that she died, but we would have killed one another. For the longest time I felt guilty after she died. There was one night that we fought so bad that she went into early labor."

I felt so bad for him. "I can't imagine you really fighting with anyone. I see your knuckles, but you're so even keeled I just can't believe and that you'd..."

"Don't think I didn't' walk away from her," he told me. "I did everything I could to avoid fighting with her, but Miriam seemed to live for it. Most of the time I say my

158

peace and move on, but she would always follow me. She was determined to have the last word, determined to be hurtful."

"That sounds like my father. I see him in you sometimes." I stroked his face and reminded him that I was listening to him attentively.

"Well, my father and my wife were very much the same and it wasn't a good thing." Jack relaxed into my touch. "They keep after you until they wear you down or, in his case, drive you to lay hands on him, which I assure you I've only done this once and, to be clear, I only shook the shit out of him. When that didn't bring satisfaction, I punched the wall. You may have noticed a new photograph hanging in a precarious spot in the downstairs hallway."

I don't know what possessed me, but I shifted the subject. "So we've established that you're open to getting married again. Do you think you'll have more children?"

"I don't know. I guess that will depend on what..." Jack abruptly stopped as if he almost said something wrong. "It depends on what she wants."

The word "She" didn't worm into my ears, it went straight to my gut like a fist. What did I expect? I tried to keep in mind that this situation with him wasn't permanent, but I couldn't help but wish it was. The word I wished so badly that he'd used was "You." I wished he would have said it depended on how many children I might want.

"I think you should insist on having at least one more," I told him.

"Is that what you want? One more?" he asked.

My nerves really knotted then. I knew I'd have ten children with him if that's what he wanted, but I kept the conversation practical. "I think Josh should have a sibling. At least one. As much as I can't stand his wife, I know that I will always have Chris. If something happens to our parents I won't be alone in the world."

"I'm an only child," Jack pointed out.

159

"And when I was little I would have envied you, but now as an adult, I see what you are missing out on and it makes me a little sad. Think about what it would be like when your dad drives you insane just to be able to pick up the phone and call someone to commiserate with you, someone who knows exactly what you're going through. That's what I have with Chris. He probably knows me and my situation better than anyone."

"Better than anyone?" Jack raised his eyebrow.

"I know what you're getting at and get your mind out of the gutter. You know me better than anyone in that regard."

Chapter 18

Dinner at Bud & Alley's would never be the same after eating there with Jack. As I had tainted the grounds at the Wesley House for him, he'd tainted the restaurant for me. His talk of what he was going to do to me under the light of the fireworks left me flushed and giddy with anticipation.

July 4th, was the last day Jack and I spoke of me leaving. I think the both of us put it completely out of our minds and lived in the moment.

The days I spent alone with Jack were amazing. The injury to my arm barely registered as more than a bee sting. Alone with him was like what I imagined a really great honeymoon to be like. The beach, relaxation, absolute adoration of the one I was with and more sex than I knew was possible, it was the time of my life.

Reflecting on my conversation about my brother knowing me better than anyone and being corrected by Jack based on his specific knowledge of me, knowledge that my brother would never possess, I realized that Jack did indeed know me better than anyone and probably better than anyone ever would. I was more than content to think of him as the last person that would ever know me like that.

It was only four days that I had Jack all to myself, but they were amazing. I missed Josh and insisted Jack bring him back. I didn't think it was fair that I'd run him out of his home despite Jack's assurances that I hadn't done that.

With Josh back, we settled into our routine of sitting on the beach and watching Josh play all over again. We snuck around to keep Josh from knowing that I was sharing his father's room. I didn't mind the sneaking around. In fact, it gave an air of adventure to our escapades. Days were fun and so were the nights. My favorite things aside of making love to Jack was the three of us playing in the surf and just sitting in the chase lounge and talking with Jack well into the wee hours of the morning.

Time flew by, but on July 19, it stopped. The phone rang in the house as we were headed in from the beach that afternoon. Jack answered it and immediately took it to another room. This wasn't out of the ordinary. He got calls about work and election stuff from time to time. While he was on the phone I took Josh upstairs to get cleaned up to go to dinner. It was supposed to be date night for the three of us, but when I saw the look on Jack's face as he stood in the doorway of the bathroom watching me help Josh out of his glued on swim trunks, I knew date night was off. One expression from him said something was terribly wrong.

"Caroline, I need to talk to you for a moment." Jack offered his hand to help me up from squatting on the floor. Jack turned his attention to Josh at the same time he helped me. "Josh, get your shower and get dressed as fast as you can."

The tone of Jack's voice was eerily calm.

I followed him into the hall before asking, "What's wrong?"

Jack didn't answer immediately. He led me into the bedroom and insisted I have a seat as he closed the door behind us. "I don't know how to tell you this."

"Just tell me." Procrastination on his part would not soften the blow he was about to deliver or lessen my confusion.

Jack walked over to the bed where I was sitting and sat down next to me. He took my hands in his and held them. He didn't look me in the face. He kept his eyes trained on my hands as he ran one of his over the back of mine. "Your father's had a heart attack. We need to leave for Atlanta."

My eyes filled and I blinked back tears. "What? He's not? I mean..." I couldn't finish my sentence for the feeling that I had been punched in the gut. I ached all the way to my core over the what ifs surrounding the news.

"Your mother wouldn't tell me anymore than he'd had the heart attack and that you needed to come quickly. She insisted that I not let you drive alone and I assured her I'd come with you."

So many thoughts, worries really, ran through my mind. "He's not dead. He can't be," I started to cry.

Jack wrapped his arms around me and kissed my forehead. "I don't know. I just know that I am so sorry and I know you want to be there so I'm going to get you there. I'll be with you the whole time if that's what you need."

Jack was right, I needed to get home. I needed to find out about my father, but I couldn't expect him to drop everything.

I wiped my eyes. "What about Josh?"

"My mother's going to meet us at my house in Tallahassee. She'll take care of Josh and I'll take care of you."

Everything was a haze. I don't remember packing. I don't remember leaving the beach house or how we got to where we were going. I don't remember much other than hugging Josh goodbye.

Ordinarily I would have memorized every detail of Jack's house in Tallahassee. I would have noticed the color, the number of windows on the front, how many trees were the in yard and all sorts of details, but I didn't. I only know that I squatted down to his level and hugged Josh on the front steps as if it might be the last time I saw him.

"I love you sweet boy and I will miss you until I see you again," I told him. I held back tears and made my eyes dance just for him.

"I love you too, Aunt CC, and I will miss you until I see you again, too." Josh was cheerful and ignorant to anything that was amiss with me. I hadn't wanted to worry him so I'd succeeded.

I clutched him through his little brown curls as he held tight around my neck. "I love you! I love you! I love you!" I said in between each kiss I planted on him, one on each cheek and one on his forehead.

Jack helped me up and I headed back to the car. I heard him behind me explaining to Josh that he'd be "staying with Grandma a few days," but we'd be back soon. Something inside me hinted that I wasn't coming back. News of my father, leaving Josh, everything felt like it was falling apart. As soon as the tires hit the pavement outside of Jack's driveway, I fell apart. My hands went to my face and I sobbed uncontrollable.

"I'm so sorry," I apologized through my fingers as I cried.

"There's nothing to be sorry about." Jack placed a hand on the back of my head and slid it down until it rested on my neck.

"There's everything to be sorry about. I'm sorry that we just had to leave Josh. I'm sorry you're having to drive me because my mother still thinks I'm a child. I'm most sorry that she didn't see fit to provide any detail of my father's condition. No, I'm beyond sorry. I'm furious. What if..."

Jack, sensible as always, rubbed my neck and shushed me. "I can't tell you what's happening or has happened with your dad. All I can tell you is that I will be there with you."

I reached around and took his hand. I held it to my chest and stared at him.

"I'm not going to let you go. I'll stay with you as long as you need me," he added.

The phrase, "Life is short," whispered through my mind. What if my father died and I didn't get to say goodbye or tell him I loved him. In that moment, with those thoughts running through my mind, I turned my eyes to Jack. I absolutely adored him and my thoughts were morphing. There was something I felt compelled to tell him. We rode in silence for miles and miles as I worked up the courage to tell him.

We were somewhere between Cordele, Georgia and Tifton before I got myself together enough and got my courage up enough to say it.

I pulled Jack's hand to my lips and kissed the back of it and then pressed it to my chest again, holding it tight with both of my hands. "Jack, can I tell you something?"

"Anything," he replied.

"I love you."

Jack took his eyes off the road and stared at me. I'm not sure what I expected, but running into the median and getting us killed wasn't it.

"Jack!" I screamed.

Jack snatched his hand from mine and jerked the steering wheel and back on the interstate we went. I'd clearly surprised him.

"I know it's early on and maybe I should hold my cards closer to my vest, but I've never said that to anyone before and...Well, you don't have to say it back. I just wanted you to know especially since you are clearly about to kill us."

Jack kept looking at me as I rambled on and we veered off the road again and again he snatched it back.

Jack got the car back on the road safely for the second time and following that there was a long period of silence. I was left wondering if I'd made a horrible mistake by telling him. I'd been keeping it to myself for so long, but feeling it to my core as I'd never felt before. Even though when working up my nerve to say it out loud, I'd told myself it didn't matter if he said it back. Me saying it to him was something I was giving him. It wasn't about me. It was because I loved him that I wanted him to know. Now that seemed like a strange cycle.

There was an exit from the interstate up ahead for a rest stop. It was well within sight when Jack broke the silence. "Do you need to use the restroom?"

That wasn't what I'd expected his next words to be and before I could force my befuddled mind to reply, Jack had the blinker on, changed lanes and was racing along the ramp toward the rest stop.

I mustered the word, "Okay," in response.

Jack whipped his Jaguar into one of the first spots we came to. "Wait here. I'll come around," he instructed me with haste in his voice.

I repeated, "Okay," and followed him with my eyes as he jumped out of the car and sprinted around to my side.

The parking spot he chose was about as far away from the building as there was. Jack held my hand as we walked from the car all the way there. I took that as a good sign. He stopped once and just looked at me, studied my face, before leading me on toward the building. I was more puzzled now than I was in the car. He walked so quickly that I could hardly keep up. The one thing I was sure of was that everything really was falling apart.

The first thing I noticed about Jack when we met back up outside of the bathrooms at the rest stop was that he appeared to have splashed water on his face. He still didn't say much on the walk back to the car.

"Are you ready?" That was all he said.

"Sure?" I replied, but the involuntary fluctuation in my voice made it sound more like a question than a statement. Jack's behavior was eating at me, but I held my tongue.

I reached for the handle of the car door about the same time as Jack. It unlatched. I heard that clicking sound that locks make, but before I could open it Jack laid a hand on the door and I heard it snap back. In the same split second that I turned my head to see what was wrong, Jack spun me and pinned me to the car. It was one fluid movement and his body was pressed to mine. He had a hand in my hair at the base of my skull and another wrapped all the way around me, securing me to him by my waist. Jack buried his face in my hair, pressing his cheek to mine and I leaned into his touch. I didn't know what to do with my arms or hands, but like an instinct I wrapped them around him.

I could feel Jack's breath on my ear as he spoke. "Not since Mary Deloach in the third grade have I told a female other than my mother that I loved her."

My breath caught in my chest and my heart stopped. I could see the cars zipping past us to reach spaces closer to the doors than us. I could also see the cars continuing on the interstate. There were horns blowing from big rigs and thunder rolling in the distance, but nothing broke my focus on Jack. His grip tightened on me and I could feel his heartbeat against me through his t-shirt, through his Polo shirt and through my clothes. I wanted him to kiss me, tell me he loved me and that everything was going to be okay.

"Remember what I told you I would to do to you? What I wanted to do to you?" Jack's nose traced over my ear.

Not only did I remember, but I felt him pressing into me. I knew what he wanted. Thoughts of everything, but him escaped me and for a moment I felt the weight of the world fall off of me.

"Ravage me," I breathed.

"Yes. I want that more so now. Do you remember what I told you under the wedding tree?"

I couldn't speak. I ached for him so badly that tears were starting to pool in my eyes.

"Sometimes an anomaly comes along. You're the anomaly. You, Caroline. I've waited for you all my life. You're the person I'd lasso the moon for."

I blinked my eyes and the tears slipped free and rolled down my cheeks. I clutched him tighter.

Jack continued, "Any man would love the way you look. You are the most stunning woman I've ever seen. The first time I looked at you it physically hurt not to be able to have you. The thing is, it's not your physical attributes that make me crave you, it's the way you love

Josh, the way you are with him, I could watch you all day. The way you were with my mother. There's a kindness to you like nothing I've ever seen, but there's also a fight in you that burns like a fire when crossed. It's a privilege that you allow me to touch you and telling you I love you is something I've fought. Everything logical says it's too soon. You're too young for me. I'm too old for you. I wondered if you could ever feel the same for me. I resisted telling you. I did, but my heart screams at my brain every single time I see you, I touch you, I hear your voice. It screams I love you. I love you, Caroline."

Jack forged his lips with mine and I was devoured. When he pulled back from me, breathless and glistening with a thin layer of perspiration, he drew my heart even closer to his. "You're who I picture coming to me beneath the wedding tree."

I held Jack's face in my hands and gazed adoringly into those blistering blue eyes of his. "I'm going to meet you under that tree one day."

Chapter 19

Back on the road I had renewed hope that my father was going to be alright. I was still worried, terribly worried, but my father was a man barely into his sixties and in relatively good health as far as I knew. A touch, a kiss, a phrase from Jack and my nerves were a little soothed, but I still longed to be with my family.

Jack kept one hand on the wheel and the other entwined with mine. Most likely, to keep me distracted from thinking about my father, Jack asked me if I'd ever been in love before.

"I thought so once," I shrugged.

"But you don't now?" he followed up.

"I know better now."

"How's that?" He took is eyes of the wheel and glanced at me.

"I was a stupid girl before." I answered, but I didn't want to talk about me. I changed the subject. "Why don't you tell me why you've never told anyone before? Have you never been in love before? And, what about Josh's mother? You never told her?"

"So many questions. I don't think I've ever really been in love before. My parents always had me so busy and focused during high school, plus I was a bit chubby. I didn't date much," Jack would have gone on, but I interrupted him.

"I can't imagine you were chubby."

"I was a full on ugly duckling, but go on."

"I grew a foot in my senior year and stretched out the fat. I had a sudden popularity. I dated around a little in college, but nothing compared to most of my friends," Jack continued to describe.

"And then there was Miriam?"

"Yes, and then there was Miriam and she put an end to everything. So, there was never a chance for me to find someone serious."

"And you never told her you loved her? I mean, you married her. How did you get around it leading up to the wedding and at the wedding? And, when she gave birth? She was okay with that?" I couldn't get over it.

"We had a microscopic engagement. She was just about showing by the time the wedding took place. When we weren't fighting and completely pissed off with one another, like on our wedding day, I was focused on finishing college and she was focused on paint colors for the baby's room, what stroller was the most expensive and scheming to extort my parents over me getting her pregnant. I would have died a thousand deaths before telling her I loved her."

"Then she died."

"Yep, then she died."

"Why not anyone after her?"

"You're after her." Jack gave my hand a squeeze.

"Yes, but there were seven years in between. What were you doing?" I just couldn't make sense of it.

"I was mostly pissed off about Miriam. Pissed off at myself because I hated her and feeling guilty because she died and I hated her. Did I mention I hated her?" Jack made fun of himself for the repetition.

"You must have liked her at some point at least enough to..." That time Jack didn't let me finish.

"Just so you know, it was twice. I *liked* her twice. That's all." Jack brought my hand to his mouth, "You know how many times I've *loved* you?" He stuck my index finger in his mouth and swirled his tongue around it. "Six the first night alone."

I let out a long exhale.

"I love you, Caroline."

Somewhere around Warner Robins our conversation tapered off. Jack encouraged me to take a little nap since we didn't know what was in store for us when we reached Atlanta. I drifted off.

"Caroline." I heard him, but barely registered it beyond a dream until he said my name again. "Caroline!"

Jack gave me a nudge. "We're coming into Atlanta. Wake up."

It was dark out. I squinted and let my seat up. Car lights whizzed by us and street lights along the interstate shown through the sunroof. The clock in the car said 10:23 p.m.

"Caroline, wake up." Jack gave me another nudge. "You're going to have to tell me where we're going. I've never driven in Atlanta before."

I saw the overhanging sign ahead. It was a sign for 285, the bi-pass around Atlanta.

"Get over!" I pointed to the inside lanes. "We've got to go through the city."

"Okay." Jack twisted in his seat and checked for traffic coming up on his side and put on the blinker.

"Stay on 75. I-85 will come into it. It's called the connector and it will take us through Atlanta."

"This is craziness." Jack floored it and the engine purred louder as we jumped to the next lane.

"Go another lane!" I watched for a spot for us to get over again.

"Okay. Okay."

On the far side of downtown, I gave instructions to take I-75 at the split. "We live in what's called Buckhead."

"I've heard of it."

A right off of I-75 north of town onto West Paces Ferry and a few turns later and we were there, pulling into my parents' driveway. The house was lit up, but that didn't mean anything. Daddy kept most of the lights on timers so the fact that half the lights in the house were on didn't mean anyone was home.

Our house wasn't grand compared to most in the area, but it wasn't the rot gut house either. It was a tad over the top for most of Atlanta, but middle grade for this area. It was a five bedroom Colonial that was built in the fifties. My parents were the second owners and they bought it in the mid-seventies. I overheard them talking about selling it in the late spring and according to Daddy the location alone pushed it well over the million dollar mark.

The driveway was long and the house sat toward the back of the acre lot. We rolled up the driveway and I was ready to jump out and run inside long before Jack shut the car off. Of course he could tell and stopped me.

"Take a moment and breathe," he insisted. "I don't know what awaits you, but no matter what, I've got you and you've got me. Now, sit here and I'll come around."

Jack's words echoed through my head as we walked toward the door. I put my key in but, before I could turn the handle, my mother snatched the door open and threw her arms around me.

"CC, the most wonderful news! It was a mild heart attack, but he's going to be okay!" Mama squeezed me tight right there in the threshold of the front door. For someone whose husband had just had a heart attack, she was overjoyed.

I was so relieved, I started with the involuntary crying again. "That's great news!

Mama quickly let go of me and became the picture of Southern hospitality as she turned her attention to Jack. She straightened her back, her blouse, pressed down her skirt and wiped back her hair from her forehead. "Jack, I'm so sorry you had to come all this way."

"It's no trouble. Glad to do it." Jack placed a hand on the small of my back and led me through the door as Mama backed out of the way. Once inside the door Mama threw her arms around him, too.

Mama backed off from Jack and looked at the both of us. She had a tendency to talk with her hands so they were flailing about. "I'm just so glad y'all are here!"

Jack sat the bags down that he'd carried in for us as I asked Mama more about Daddy.

"Well, I know it's late, but can we go see him?" I asked her.

"Oh, no, they've got him scheduled for one of those angioplasty procedures early tomorrow morning so he needs to get his rest tonight." Mama waved away the notion of going to the hospital to see him right then. "Are y'all hungry?"

Mama started toward the kitchen and Jack and I followed her.

Jack answered her. He said he was starving. We'd driven straight through and hadn't stopped for dinner. I wasn't concerned with my stomach. I hadn't thought a thing about food since the phone call first came. "Is anyone with him?"

"Chris is there," she replied.

Mama made Jack a sandwich and I had a few chips. We continued to discuss the situation with my father, but Mama assured us there was absolutely nothing to worry about.

"These things are about as routine as removing an ingrown toenail. Now, Jack, I hope you don't mind, but I put you in Chris's old room."

Before Jack could ask anything, I added to Mama's mention of accommodations. "It's right next to my room and they share a Jack and Jill bathroom."

Mama sometimes tries to be funny, but most of the time it comes out as awkward. "Except in this case it's a Jack and CC bathroom."

It was almost midnight and it had been a long day for all of us so we agreed to turn in for the night.

I showered first and then Jack, each of us leaving the door between the rooms and the bathroom open. The days of modesty were long gone between us, except for using the actual toilet and that was something I couldn't bring myself to do in front of anyone, ever.

Jack emerged from the bathroom shirtless, in boxers and fresh from the shower. He was still towel drying his hair when he walked into my bedroom. "So this is where you grew up?"

"Yep. All my life with the exception of college, of course."

I was sorting things from my suitcase out into my chest of drawers and closet when Jack came in. He approached me and caught me with the towel around me like a rope.

"So this room is above the kitchen?" he asked.

"No," I twisted in the grasp of him and the towel. "It's above my parents' room."

Even flat footed, Jack loomed over me by a good five inches. "Then I guess you'll have to be quiet," Jack teased.

I bit my lip to keep from giggling.

"Let me get that for you." Jack leaned closer.

"What?"

"That lip of yours."

"My goodness, Senator Belgrave."

"Stop calling me 'Senator Belgrave' or you won't be able to keep quiet and I won't be able to look at your mother at breakfast tomorrow morning."

I backed Jack up to the edge of the bed. "I don't think I thanked you properly for bringing me home."

I studied the few lines Jack was starting to get around his eyes, likely sun damage. Drinking him in before I kissed him, I just couldn't help but think how perfect he was. Height, build, the strength he held me with, the way his hair fell over his head in dark waves, he was so mesmerizing. In that moment, I couldn't imagine a day that I wouldn't love him.

Thank goodness I'd moved my queen sized bed home from college because there was no way Jack and I would have fit in that full that I grew up in. Plus, the full sized bed was a hand me down from my grandparents' guest room. Just a look at it and it went to squeaking. There would have been no way to have been quiet in it.

Jack's fingers locked in mine over my head and softer than he'd ever been before he grated against me. He was quiet and as respectful as one could be while doing that to one's daughter right above their head. With every arch of his back and dipping of his hips he ground into me and it was tender and exquisite all at once. I drug my calf muscles over his back, down his glutes and over the back of his thigh. Then I brought them back up again while matching him with every movement. Our rhythm was in sync and I gripped my fingers around his and pressed my palms to his.

Even once we were done and totally spent, I wanted to stay entangled with Jack. With his arms around me, I laid my head on his chest where I could hear his heart sprinting well past the finish line. I draped my body half across his. That was the most comfortable spot on Earth.

"Why do you love me?" Jack asked.

I knew the answer, but it took me a moment to form the words. "I love the way you are with Josh. I know you doubt yourself because you lost him that day, but if you could see what I see, you'd know you are a great father. It's the way you are with him that is the absolute sexiest thing about you. Your looks are just a bonus. It's your heart and your brain that light a fire in me. You're like no man I've ever known," I paused for a moment as the memories of what brought us there today came rushing back. "Short of my father," I added.

I fell asleep tied up in Jack's arms and awoke in the same position at 6:00 a.m. Jack and I woke to Mama knocking on the door. We scrambled like teenagers not wanting to be caught and ever fearful that she was going to open the door and come on in.

By 7:00 a.m. we were at the hospital in time to see Daddy before he was wheeled back. The entire family was there, except Becky and Bailey.

"Don't worry about a thing," my father told me. "Everything's going to be just fine."

Mama had said the same thing to me the night before, but I had an uneasy feeling. It might have been a run of the mill procedure for the doctors there, but it wasn't a run of the mill thing for me to have happening to my father.

Chapter 20

The angioplasty went fine.

"There was a small blockage, but we pushed through. We put in a stint so we'll keep him over night again. Other than that Mr. Collier should be right as rain in no time at all," the doctor explained to the handful of us that were waiting.

I couldn't help but think how young he looked. Thick black rimmed glasses, very military issued looked too big for his gaunt face. He wasn't as tall as I was and, if he was a day older than I was, then I would be surprised. Boyish charm and gapped smile, the picture before me was distracting and not in a comforting, lending of confidence kind of way.

"So he can come home tomorrow?" Mama asked, barely able to contain her enthusiasm over the news.

"If everything goes according to plan, I don't see why not." The doctor had trouble keeping eye contact. He seemed to prefer looking people in the nose rather than the eye.

It wasn't very long before they wheeled Daddy back into his room where we'd all held vigil. He was a little groggy and pale, but the doctor assured us he was as normal as one could be under the circumstances.

During the hour Daddy was in the operating room and while Jack took Mama to get a cup of coffee, Chris and I had an opportunity to clear the air. It was the first time I'd seen him since the night Daddy threw Becky out of the beach house in Santa Rosa.

Chris began by apologizing and I accepted, but went on to explain, "I don't particularly want to talk about her. I know she's your wife, but I'm not taking the way she treats me anymore."

"I understand," Chris hung his head.

"I'm serious. I've turned the other cheek long enough. I did my part to keep the peace and I'm done.

I'm a grown adult and I deserve respect just as much as the next person so if she can't be civil to me then she can keep her mouth shut. You can tell her or I will. Furthermore, since it is my parents' home and I'm not allowed to say who comes and goes, I am asking for you not to visit when I am home from school anymore. I should be able to visit my parents without her supervision. I would love to see Bailey, but every time I came home during college y'all were there and she made it miserable for me to come home. Finally, I stopped coming home so I wouldn't have to deal with her. I kept thinking you would notice and say something, but you didn't."

"No, that's fine. You're right. I'm sorry I..."

"I know." I went over and took a seat on the arm of the chair Chris was sitting in. "It's not like she treats you much better or listens to you."

"Yeah, I had a lot of time to talk to Dad last night and he said the same thing. He said life's too short to put up with someone."

"Is that what you do? Put up with her?"

Chris shifted his posture and avoided saying the words out loud. Silence hung in the air with nothing more than the background noises of the busy hospital. Finally Chris gave a hint of his true feelings toward Becky. "I don't know if I'd miss her if she was gone or if I'd just feel relieved."

Chris stared blankly at his hands. That was the most negative thing I'd ever heard him say about her. I mean, that night at the beach he threatened to leave her to find her own way home, but something truly negative about the way he felt about her, this was a first.

I wrapped my arm around him. "You know, there are worse things than divorce."

"I just don't want to leave Bailey with her. As long as I'm there Bailey knows me and not just as a picture of me that her mother will paint. If you think she's horrible as a wife, and as a sister-in-law, she'll be that much worse as an ex-wife and former sister-in-law. You won't have to deal with her anymore, but I will and Bailey will."

"Then as for custody of Bailey. Make Becky an offer she can't refuse." I didn't know what that might be but it was the best I had.

"What's that?"

"She's your wife, you figure it out. What's her weakness?"

"Money."

"Then offer to pay whatever amount child support would be, give her the house and her car and see if she bites. I mean, if you're serious about getting out."

"And if I gave her all that how would I support Bailey? I can't afford two house payments." Chris straightened up and looked at me.

"You could always move in with Mom and Dad. They've got that big old house and it's basically empty with just the two of them there. It's not like they couldn't use some help around there. The house is paid for so you could offer them some toward the utilities and taxes. Surely you can come up with that."

Chris looked hopeful. A moment passed and he changed the subject. "So what's the deal with you and pretty boy?"

"He's not a pretty boy." My cheeks flashed red and I scooted off of the arm of the chair and on to my feet.

"CC, come on now. Everyone sees the way you two look at one another. You can't tell me you're just the nanny." Chris wasn't letting up.

"Stop," I pleaded, hiding my face in my hands and shielding my embarrassment. Talking about boys was not something I did with my brother.

"What?" Chris joked. "We can talk about my wife, but we can't talk about...what do you call him?"

My embarrassment multiplied as the phrase, "Senator Belgrave," and the context in which I referred to Jack that way crossed my mind. I tried to wipe away that thought and told Chris, "I call him Jack."

"Way to go, smart ass. You know what I mean."

I fidgeted with my hair and tried to regain my composure. I distracted myself by straightening the pillows on the stiff vinyl couch on the other side of where the bed normally sat.

"Oh my!" Chris's voice took on an air of excitement. I turned around to see him taking a long look at me. "I don't know that I've ever seen you like this before."

"Like what?" I squinted and studied Chris curiously.

"In love," Chris stated matter of fact-like.

I didn't say anything and Chris pounced on that. "You're not denying it!"

"Well, I'm not going to lie."

Our conversation came to a halt when Mama and Jack returned with their coffee. It wasn't long after that that the nurses wheeled Daddy in and the doctor followed ten minutes later.

It was hard seeing Daddy laying there in the hospital gown so weak. I'd never seen my father sick a day in his life. He'd always been an invincible, giant of a man in my eyes. I had to dab back tears when I looked at him. Jack noticed and was quick to take my hand.

"I've got you," he whispered.

A look passed between us, an unspoken I love you, thank you and I couldn't do this without you from me to him. Jack nodded and gave my hand a gentle squeeze. If he ever asked me again why I loved him, I would describe this moment. It was the way he made me feel safe in my darkest moment, the moment I saw my father as fragile. My first instinct was to bury my head in his chest and cry, but a look and a touch from him gave me the confidence not to let my family see me scared and afraid. It gave me the confidence not to mourn for my father when he wasn't dead.

After the doctor left and Daddy started to sound more coherent, Mama showered him with kisses and relayed the doctor's words. "Right as rain in a few days," she repeated.

We all congratulated Daddy, even Jack, who Daddy looked at curiously.

"He brought CC as soon as I called," Mama explained, noticing Daddy's face. "He's been so sweet to stay."

"Really?" Daddy questioned. He shifted to pull up all of the covers on the bed to make sure he was completely covered in front of Jack.

Jack was still very much a stranger to Daddy, but Mama had welcomed him in like a new member of the family.

"You need to hurry up and get well. Caroline tells me you're a huge fan of UGA football so I know you don't want to miss the opening game." Jack made a feeble attempt at small talk. "She said you've been a season ticket holder since the dawn of time. Plus, you won't want to miss my gators beating you all."

"Can you imagine it's been a year already since the Olympics?" I asked, doing my best to save everyone from the awkwardness. Daddy hated the Florida Gators with a passion. We didn't want him to get all stewed up over football.

"A year? Hum. It seems like yesterday." Chris went along with my diversion.

Daddy's attention was then turned to Chris. "You need to go home and get some rest."

"What about tonight? Do you need me to come back?" Chris asked Daddy.

"No, I think you've done your time. I think its CC's turn to stay," Daddy gave me a wink. "I think we've got some catching up to do."

While Daddy was giving me a wink, Jack started to grip my hand. When Chris started to walk out, Jack insisted we see him to his car. No sooner had the car door closed and Chris started the engine did Jack question me about staying over at the hospital that night.

"Don't get me wrong, I totally understand, but please don't. You can't leave me at the house with your mother by myself. It's just..."

"Uncomfortable? Like July the 4th with your father was a picnic? You'll be fine and I doubt you'll have to fight my mother off," I reminded him.

"Point taken, but I do it under protest."

I couldn't help but laugh at Jack. "I love you. I love you so much." The laughter stopped because suddenly, what was coming to mind wasn't so funny anymore. "So much that I'm wondering what I'm going to do when I have to go back to spending nights without you."

I frowned a little and Jack took me in his arms. Jack rested his chin on the top of my head. My nose nestled near his Adam's apple and I breathed him in. As long as I lived I would never forget his scent.

"I don't want to think about that yet," he sighed.

On the way back to my father's hospital room, Jack insisted we stop by the gift shop. From the gift shop, Jack purchased a deck of cards and what he called "trash mags".

"You'll need something to take the edge off of the boredom tonight," he said to me as he handed the cashier his money. He then indicated to her that he needed his change back in quarters.

In the hallway outside of Daddy's room, Jack handed me the quarters. "Put these somewhere in case you need to raid the vending machines tonight."

Jack seemed to know a thing or two about staying at the hospital. I wondered if that was from when Josh was born and he had to say with Miriam. I wasn't quite curious enough to ask.

"Thank you, but I'm sure I won't need four dollars' worth of Coke and candy bars." Despite my reluctance, Jack put the change in my hand and insisted that I take it.

"You never know." Jack smiled and refused to take the money back.

In the room Jack put the magazines in the window sill and I put the change in my purse. Mama was combing Daddy's hair when we walked in, but she finished by the time Jack got the cards out. Jack started with the deck of cards, opening them and sorting out the jokers.

"So," he started, "I figure since you're stuck here you might as well have some fun, if you're up for it of course. We'll start with something simple, like Go Fish."

The entire time Jack was talking he was shuffling the cards on the meal tray that rolled over Daddy's hospital bed.

"Okay, but let's skip to Gin Rummy," Daddy insisted as he pressed the buttons and elevated himself into a more upright position.

Mama was quick to caution him, "Hun, you don't need to exert yourself."

"Oh stop it!" He shirked away from her. "I'm not dying and it's not like I'm going to be playing Slap-Jacks with Bailey."

I was thumbing through one of the magazines when Jack mentioned my name. He called me by the nickname my parents used, which was something he rarely did, and that got my attention. "CC, come on. Cut the cards. I'm dealing you in."

Daddy instructed Jack to deal Mama in too. "We'll all play."

God bless her, Mama was terrible at games. She always lost and therefore she almost always refused to play. At Daddy's request, Mama took a seat on the edge of the bed and indulged him. Jack dealt us all a hand and the four of us played Rummy until the dieticians brought in Daddy's lunch and ran us off of our make-shift card table. In spite of our circumstances we were all having a really good time. Even Mama won a few hands.

Being the gentleman he was, Jack bought lunch for Mama and me. Since Mama wouldn't leave before visiting hours were over, lunch came from the hospital cafeteria. While there, Jack picked up two packs of M&Ms

for each of us. After lunch we commenced with the card games again. This time we played poker and used the M&Ms as chips. It was my first time playing poker so when I won twice in a row they chalked it up to beginners luck. When I won the third time in a row, Daddy and Jack razzed me about lying regarding it being my first time.

"Next she'll want to play for money," Jack chided me.

"You did give me a stack of quarters." I punched Jack playfully.

The four of us had a great time that afternoon. I loved how Jack fit right in with us. I loved how both Mama and Daddy seemed to genuinely like Jack and seemed interested in getting to know him that afternoon. All of that made Daddy's conversation with me that evening surprising.

Daddy didn't wait too long after Mama and Jack left to approach the subject of me and Jack. He started with basically the same question Chris had. "So, what's with you and the Senator?"

I tried dodging the question, but Daddy would have none of it. I had to say something. Chris knew. For all I knew, he went straight home and told Becky and she'd tell just for spite. With reluctance to confess anything was going on at all, I gave a watered down version. "We're dating."

"You're living together," Daddy promptly corrected me.

"No, and everything is temporary. I'm starting school soon." I hoped Daddy didn't hear the hurt in my voice that came with any thought of leaving Jack and Josh.

"Really? The way the two of you look at one another, and hang on each other's every word and each other's every move, doesn't look so temporary."

"Daddy, please, you need to rest." I moved to fluff his pillow, but he didn't budge more than to grab my hand.

"Do you begin to know who you're dealing with?" Daddy flipped my arm around and showed me the light scab and reddened skin forming the scar around it from the run in with Jack's father. "Are people who will do this to you who you want in your life? Your mother told me what happened, but from the looks of this you sugar coated it."

I snatched my arm away and clutched it to my chest. "Jack didn't do this to me!" I was adamant and offended that my father would imply such about him. "Jack is amazing and..."

"That he is," my father interrupted me. "He's so great that he's lined up to be the next president of our country. Do you honestly think that the people who've aligned all of this for him will allow you to get in the way?"

"Get in the way?" I didn't understand.

"You're twenty-two. You'll be twenty-six at the time of the election. This day and age, you are too young to be taken seriously as a first lady. So," Daddy allowed his eyes linger on my arm, "you think they'll risk all that they've put into him and allow some girl to muck it up for him? For them?" Daddy shook his head.

I was so stunned. My heart was breaking. I couldn't believe what Daddy was saying.

"Even if somehow he can protect you and you make the cut, sure there've been first wives before that were in their twenties, but that was when the president's personal life was off limits. Jackie Kennedy was thirty-one and do you know the huge deal that was made of her age? How she was hounded by the press for every move she made? And, that was the press from the sixties. Your life would never be your own. Every move you make would be scrutinized. I'm sure you think you love him, but do you think your love for him will survive that? The farther he climbs toward the presidency the farther away he will be pulled from you and, in the end, he probably won't get elected and where will you be?"

"Daddy, please," I wiped my eyes and flopped back into the side chair. "That's so far down the road and we're just..."

"Dating, I know, you said." Daddy reached a hand over to me. "I don't mean to make you cry or upset you, CC, but this is a very big deal. I've read a lot about him since you've been down there. He is a great guy and he's electable. Of course I'd love for you to end up with someone like him, if all of this other wasn't involved. Everyone's got a very high opinion of him, but just having you around is a liability for his career, his future. If he's photographed with you and it gets out that he's dating a twenty-two year old that looks like you, he won't be taken seriously anymore. Every good thing he's done will be turned on its head and he will be finished. You know how they talk about our current president and his inability to keep his pants up. Is that what you want for him?"

"No," I sniffled.

"Baby, under any other circumstances, I'd pick him for you, I swear, but you're just too young and I don't want the baggage that comes with him for you. I also don't want him to throw away his future for what might be a fleeting romance. I think if you love him, if you love yourself, you need to end it."

Daddy didn't say anything more on the subject. He just left me with my thoughts which were stubborn, dug in ideas of how Jack and I could make it work.

Chapter 21

Somewhere between dream and reality, rolling over in Jack's bed beneath his arms and squirming to get comfortable in the hospital chair that made an obscene noise every time I moved, a beeping noise invaded my ears. It was incessant, one long drawn out beep. Suddenly I wasn't between anything. I was there in the room with nurses and anyone else in a uniform rushing in.

"Ma'am, please," one pushed by me as I was getting to my feet, blocking me with her arm as she rounded Daddy's bed. "Get her out of here," she screamed to those who were her subordinates.

Coming to and getting my bearings, I recognized the noise, but not because I'd ever heard it in person before. It was the noise from every T.V. show or movie that dealt with hospitals. It was the sound of a flat line. Daddy's heart had stopped.

Medical terms flew left and right as I was pushed out of the room.

"Is he going to be alright?" I shouted above them.

"We're doing all we can, Miss, all we can." The nurse in the pink scrubs said as she gave me one last gentle push and then pushed the door to where there was only a little crack left.

The beeping persisted and I could hear it all the way in the hall. I could hear it over the doctor or nurse or whoever it was that was barking out the orders trying to save my father. I peeped through the crack until the same nurse saw me and shut it the door completely. Right in my face, she shut it.

Even through the closed door I could hear the sound of the flat line. Then, it stopped. The door opened and the same lady in pink frowned, tilted her eyes to the floor and shook her head. A voice behind her said, "Call it," and another said, "Time of death 3:03 a.m."

3:03 a.m. that was the time my world came crashing down. It didn't just hit the floor. It went straight to Hell.

My legs went weak and I started down. Luckily the nurse caught me. She was a heavy set lady fully capable of holding my weight and hers. Most of those who entered the room passed us. Each offered their condolences, but I didn't acknowledge them. The nurse continued to hold me and I clung to her and sobbed as if I were a child clinging to its mother until I remembered my mother. My heart broke for all of us, but for my mother most of all.

I snatched back and covered my mouth. "Oh my God," came out muffled. My eyes went wide and the tears still fell. "I need to use a phone."

"Of course," she said. She hadn't taken her hands off of me. She was probably still scared I was going to faint. Cautiously, she started to lead me down the hall and offered to call anyone I needed her to call.

I wiped my eyes and focused on putting one foot in front of the other. "I should be the one to call."

The nurse showed me to a patient's room that was empty. "You can use this room as long as you need to. I'll be outside if you need me, just yell. My name's Trudy."

"Thank you." I tried to smile as I said the words, but my face just wouldn't. A couple of blinks of gratitude were all I could manage.

Trudy stepped out of the room as I made my way across to the bedside table. A phone waited there and I picked up the receiver. I dialed Chris's number and waited.

"Hello?!" A very curt Becky answered.

I tried not to judge as that's how most anyone would answer the phone when woken in the middle of the night.

"Becky, it's CC." I didn't get another word out before I heard the dial tone. She hung up.

If it weren't so typically Becky to be nasty at every opportunity the phrase "I can't believe her" would have crossed my mind, but this was so true to form. I dialed the number again. I hoped Chris would answer, but this time Becky just picked up the receiver and laid it down.

My plan was to call Chris and have him go over and get Mother. I wanted him to break the news to her or bring her to the hospital and I would do it with him. I didn't want to tell my mother over the phone that Daddy had died. All of this was foiled by Becky and I hated her now more than ever. I hated her so much that it almost clouded my grief. I wanted to scream in the phone just what I thought she was, but I remembered where I was. All I could do was cry over a mix of frustration and the ache of losing my father.

The fury and the ache went all the way to my bones. It took me quite a while before I calmed down enough to do what I knew needed to be done. I ran my hands roughly over my face and smeared what little, if any, makeup was left all the way down to my neck. I rubbed my eyes again and struggled to see the numbers on the phone through the mixture of tears and mascara. I plucked out my home phone number, the number to my parents' house.

Knowing that it wasn't possible, I prayed Jack would pick up. I knew his manners were too impeccable to answer a phone at someone else's house, but that didn't keep me from hoping.

It rang a few times and my mother picked up. Even roused from her sleep, she answered more pleasantly than Becky.

"Hello?" Her sweet voice blistered my ears with the dread of knowing the news that had to be delivered.

"Mama, it's me," I said slowly, so slowly that she didn't let me finish.

"CC, what's wrong?" Mama was now alert and demanding.

I didn't completely answer her. "Please wake Jack and have him drive you to the hospital."

"CC, you tell me what's the matter!" Mama's voice trembled.

"Just have Jack bring you and come quickly. Please, Mama."

"Okay."

Trudy told me I could sit in the room with Daddy while I waited, but I didn't want to remember him like that. She then offered me a private waiting room.

"No, I'll be fine right here," I told her as I slumped down and back against the wall. "I want my mother to be able to find me when she arrives."

Even though I dreaded it more than I'd ever dreaded anything, I didn't want her to hear it from anyone else.

I was sitting against the wall with my knees drawn up when I heard my mother call my name as she came running down the hall. Jack chased after her. I jumped up and caught her in my arms before she could charge through the door. I'd gotten a glimpse of him, just enough to know I wanted to prepare her for seeing him lying there like he was.

"Mama, I'm so sorry," I held her and cried.

"Sorry for what, Caroline?" Mama pulled back.

I hadn't said it out loud and refused to tell her on the phone, but I thought she would have figured it out. Maybe she did and she was in denial. Maybe she just had to be told flat out.

I felt Jack's hand at the small of my back. He steadied me and, with his touch, I found the courage to tell my mother that my father had died.

"How? Why?" she asked, but I didn't have any answers.

"I don't know." No one had told me anything. "All I know is that he was asleep and then..." I broke down.

"Caroline, tell me what happened!" Mama pleaded.

"I don't know," I cried. "I don't know."

"Mrs. Collier," a male voice spoke softly as he approached.

Mama turned and I looked past her.

Jack's arm went around my waist and he pulled me into his side. "I'm so sorry, Caroline. No matter what, remember, I've got you."

My father's words ran through my mind. "End it," he'd told me. I glanced at Jack and couldn't imagine it.

Jack held me as I started to cry again. So many conflicting emotions were fighting inside of me.

The last words I spoke to my father also ran through my mind. I remembered telling him, "I don't want to talk to you anymore." He didn't let me finish my sentence and say that I didn't want to talk to him anymore about Jack. Instead, the memory I was left with was that I told him I didn't want to talk to him anymore.

The doctor explained to my mother, "As best we can tell, Mr. Collier suffered a major stroke. We will be happy to perform an autopsy..."

"I don't understand." Mama rung her hands. "Y'all said he would be fine."

I stepped forward to comfort her and show solidarity. I took her hands in mine. Jack stayed by my side. Where I went, he went. He had a hand on me the entire time.

"Sometimes things are out of our control, Ma'am. Again, we'll be happy to perform an autopsy..."

Mama really snapped then, "You'll be happy to do to an autopsy? Excuse me? Who says such things?"

"I'm sorry," the doctor stuttered and repeated himself. "I'm so sorry. I just meant..."

"No, you will not do an autopsy. You will not cut him open and..." Mama broke down at that point.

Jack then spoke for us, something Chris should have been there to do. "Could you just give us a little bit?"

191

"Certainly," the doctor then slinked away in the direction from which he came.

"Mrs. Collier, I know this isn't something you want to think about, but perhaps you need to have the autopsy done. Then you would know what happened," Jack suggested.

"No." Mama relaxed and the reality of the situation started to set in. She started to gasp as the devastating loss overwhelmed her. "Oh God! Oh God!"

Mama jerked away from me and rushed into the room. She threw herself over Daddy.

Jack pulled me into him and whispered, "Let her say goodbye."

At a decent hour, Mama called one of the prominent funeral homes and, while they were on their way to get Daddy and while we waited, Mama called Chris. She asked him to meet us at the house. We had a funeral to plan.

"I feel like I'm circling a drain," I described to Jack.

Jack was throwing back the covers and I was finishing up in the bathroom. The door was open between us. I leaned over the sink and inspected my puffy eyes. I'd hardly gone five minutes all day without crying and, looking at myself now, I could see and feel the tears rising for another go.

"I was there. I saw almost everything and, what I didn't see, I heard. My brain says it's so, but my heart just cannot comprehend. I can't believe he's gone. So, I'm circling, caught between fact and fiction."

I washed my face and studied my reflection again. The cool water didn't improve anything.

Jack finished in the bedroom and walked over to me. He stood behind me and wrapped his arms around my waist and I wrapped mine around his.

"Of course everyone says it, but I'd give anything for five more minutes with him." I leaned my head back into Jack's shoulder.

"Why just five minutes?" He asked as he leaned his cheek against the side of my head.

I looked past my reflection in the mirror to his. I hesitated with my answer and Jack prodded me.

"Tell me." He leaned his nose into my hair. Freshly washed and dried and scented with shampoo, he breathed it in. "Tell me," he whispered a second time.

"I didn't exactly leave things on the best of terms with him." I exhaled and let my eyes drift back.

"You had a fight with him?"

I opened my eyes to find Jack looking at me in the mirror. Every time I looked at him I could hear Daddy's telling me to end it.

"Not so much a fight as a disagreement." I went on to tell Jack specifically what I'd said about not wanting to talk to him anymore and Jack didn't let it go. I ended up telling him all about Daddy's demand for me to end things with him and why.

"He said if the wrong people found out about us it would end your career. Any chance of you being president one day would be over. He said the press would hound us over our age difference and nothing else would matter. He made me look at my arm and told me that the people who got you where you are wouldn't let some girl stop them. Showing me the scar on my arm," and I looked at it as I spoke, "this would be nothing, compared to what they could do. He implied they would hurt me, really hurt me."

Jack let go of me and stepped away.

"You know I love you," I said to him.

"Yes, of course," Jack turned and said over his shoulder as he walked into the bedroom.

I followed and Jack didn't stop until he sat down on the edge of the bed. He dropped his head in his hands. Starting with his face he ran them up and over the back of his head. His elbows propped on his knees and his hands cupped around his neck, he sat there and it appeared the weight of the world was bearing down on him.

"What is it?" I fell on my knees in front of him and pleaded for him to look at me.

"Your father's parting advice to you was to end it with me," he shook his head.

"Yes, but..."

"I'll go tomorrow morning."

"What? Why?" I stammered, gasping through the words, taking another stab to my heart. How much more could I bear?

"Because, Caroline, you'll never get past what he said. He's already whispering in your ear every time you look at me isn't he?"

I covered my mouth. How did he know?

"Please, no. You said..."

"I said I'll meet you under the wedding tree one day and I want that, but it's only been two months. You can still get over this or maybe one day the whispering will stop or maybe it won't. Maybe your father was right. Maybe we have to end it for now."

"But you're leaving me? Now?"

Jack grabbed me and to the floor we went. He kissed me feverishly, more passionately that I knew was imaginable. "I don't want to leave you. I never want to leave you," Jack panted in between kisses. "Never."

"Then don't." I tore his t-shirt off of him and we made love like there was no tomorrow.

I tossed and turned and hardly slept all night. I couldn't shake the heartsickness over my father or his warning over Jack. When I did dream, one was of my father sitting up in that bed after he'd laid cold and luckily my mind jerked awake before that ended as badly as I expect it would have. The next dream was of Jack and I being chased. No faces, no idea if it was animal or human, just something chasing us. I worried these were signs. I could not shake the worry or the dread.

In the morning, I began the discussion again. We lay in bed and I knew what was ahead of us. I had to help Mama plan the funeral. I knew who all would be invited plus those who came from seeing the obituary in the newspaper. Daddy knew everyone from the governor right down to the man and his family who cleaned the houses before they were sold. He knew every real estate broker in Atlanta, every contractor and every architect around and they knew him. My father knew everyone.

"You can't come to the funeral," I said very reluctantly.

"You don't want me there?" Jack questioned.

"Of course I do. I need you there, but I don't want to ruin anything for you. You were right about him whispering in my ear. Since I first laid eyes on you at the hospital yesterday morning all I could think about was how great you are and how I can't be the one that holds you back. There'll be a number of state politicians there. You would run into someone and they'd want to know how you know him and lying and being found out would be worse than telling the truth from the get go. News outlets will be there and you cannot be photographed with me."

"So this is how it's going to be?" he asked.

"I think it may be the way it has to be," I sighed.

Chapter 22

Thank Heavens Millie walked in when she did. The train of remembrance I was on was about to take me farther down the tracks toward the worst day of my life, the day we buried my father and the day I let Jack go. The bitter memories had already started to seep in by the time Millie got my attention.

"Hey! What are you doing?" Millie must have seen the tears starting to form in my eyes. "Are you alright? Gabe said you were a little off this morning."

I was sitting on the bed in the Magnolia room, one of our guest rooms, when Millie found me. I glanced at my watch, wondering how long I'd been sitting there. Two hours, that's how long it had been since the trip down memory lane began. The last thing I remembered of my morning was fluffing the pillows for the bed. When Millie spoke and snapped me back to reality, I found myself hugging one of the pillows.

"It's nothing I won't get over." I wiped my eyes and stood up from the bed as I told my lie. The truth was, it was something I was never going to get over as evidenced by my reaction to his photograph in the paper.

"You know, I can always tell when you're lying to me. It's a gift." Millie tried to lighten my mood and pry at the same time.

"A gift, huh?" I sucked up the fluids compacting in my face. "You're so talented."

The truth was being able to catch me in a lie, which I rarely told, was her gift. She'd seen right through me the first time we met. She asked me basically the same thing that morning as she repeated then. "Are you alright?"

I let out a huff of air with the roll of my lips and I shook my head. Millie reached over and took the pillow from me and put it in its proper place on the bed. Then she pressed out the back of her skirt and took a seat at the foot. By the look of her, she'd been to court that morning: business suit, hair pulled up in a bun and she still had on her heels. Millie in heels was a rarity.

"I've got all day," Millie said. She patted the same spot on the bed where I'd just been seated. She also handed me the newspaper she must have dug out of the office trashcan where I'd tossed it. "Gabe said you looked at this as if you'd seen a ghost. Why don't you tell me about the ghost?"

I took the paper and unfolded it. I pointed to Jack's photo. He's no ghost. He's very much alive. I dropped my head in my hands. "He's the one. He's my version of Gabe."

"Ah...the Senator..." Millie exhaled with the light bulb in her head going off like a blue light on a cop car.

"Yep, the Senator." I mimicked with my own long drawn out exhale. I flopped back on the bed.

"Says he's going to be playing a charity golf event at *the* country club in Augusta." Millie laid the paper on my chest.

I'd read it earlier so I knew what she meant when she emphasized the word "the". It was the be-all end-all of country clubs. Presidents played there, not just one but several, and only the richest of the rich men were invited in as members.

"I've got a client that's a member. He could get us in. I mean, if you want to go," Millie flopped back on the bed next to me. "We should go."

"And why would we do that?" I rolled my head over and faced away from her.

"Because, you need to go." Millie locked her hand in mine.

"Is that so?" Gravity pulled a tear down my cheek.

"It is." Millie gave my hand a squeeze.

I turned my face back toward her. "I don't think I can ever face him again."

"Well, there's thinking a thing and there's knowing it and I think it's high time you knew it. Come

197

on, CC, you've been pining away for him since the day I met you. I think it's high time you go get him back."

"You sure have a lot of confidence in my abilities."

"Have you looked in the mirror?" Millie smiled.

"You say that, but he's the only person's who's ever looked past my packaging so I don't think I can rely on my pretty face this time."

"Don't be silly." Millie sat up. "The tournament is on Friday so I'll secure the invite and all you need to do is pick out what you're going to wear."

"Millie, seriously, I can't go. We have a big wedding and a full house here at the inn this weekend. I can't leave Gabe."

"Please, I'll get Aunt Gayle to fill in for you." Millie dismissed my concerns.

Aunt Gayle was Millie's aunt and she took about as much interest in the place as the rest of us, she just wasn't on the payroll.

Gabe called up the stairs, "I have a new recipe for you girls to sample!"

Mine and Millie's conversation was revisited later in the afternoon when Millie found me in one of the cabins. I was dusting and making sure everything was in good working order, fresh towels, mints on pillows, that sort of thing. I was alone with my thoughts and trying fiercely not to think about Jack, but I was struggling. I could not get his face out of my head and the fear out of the pit of my stomach. The time for me to try to get him back was long since passed.

In walked Millie. "The tickets will be waiting on us at the gate Friday morning. Aunt Gayle is on board and Gabe is fine with us going." She was proud of herself.

"Honestly, we were only together for two months. He probably doesn't even remember me."

"Shut up!" Milled stomped her foot. "Just stop with all of the low self-esteem bullshit! Get yourself together. You're better than this!"

"Fine." I rolled my eyes.

"You're welcome." Millie tilted her head and waited.

"Thank you," I said about as reluctantly as I'd said the word, "Fine."

"Good, now we'll leave here around 10 a.m. Friday morning. You have something to wear right?" Millie looked me up and down. I was taller than she was and a tad more filled out so if she was offering to loan me something that would never do.

"I'm sure I have something." That wasn't an understatement. The perfect thing popped in my head. I'd wear one of the dresses Jack had bought me all those years ago when he took me shopping. I'd never worn them, but I'd carted them home from the beach that summer, to my parents' house, to Mercer and then here to the home I'd made for myself at Seven Springs. I'd been saving them for a special occasion and I guess the prospect of seeing him again was as special as it would get.

It wasn't a part of my duties to work in the restaurant, but I worked until the restaurant closed that night. I helped out wherever I could just to pass the time. I plated up food, refilled glasses and cashed out some of the guests. I still didn't want to be alone with my thoughts. I'd relived my summer with Jack and I was fine with the memories stopping there. As long as I kept busy my mind stayed occupied with other things, but as soon as I crawled into bed that night, in the stillness of the old hotel, there was no place left for my thoughts to hide.

I reached over to the night stand and picked up the newspaper. I unfolded it and gazed at his photograph. He hadn't aged a day. Just looking at his picture made me ache for him. I laid the paper to the side and reached in the drawer of the night stand. I took out a scrap of notebook paper that I hadn't unfolded in a few years, but tonight I unfolded it and read it.

July 22, 1997

Caroline,

Don't think for one moment that I won't fight for you. I know what I want and it's you, Caroline. I want you, but I understand what your father was saying. For us to be together there will be sacrifices and consequences. I know what I'm willing to sacrifice and that I'm prepared for the consequences. I think you need to take some time and decide what consequences you can live with and what you are willing to sacrifice for your happiness. You know where to find me and I hope you do come find me. Take as much time as you need and, know that I meant what I said, I hope to see you under the wedding tree one day. Josh and I will be waiting.

Yours always,

Jack

Jack stayed until we left for the funeral and when I got back that was the note I found from him. He left the ball in my court, but I didn't know what to do with it. I wanted to chase after him, but my father's words wouldn't stop playing like a record with a skip. Daddy had a point and I didn't want to cost Jack what he'd been working for all of his life. The thing that I sacrificed was my own happiness and I sacrificed it for him. I wanted him to be happy and I wanted him to get all that he deserved in life even if that meant letting him go.

I never changed my mind about wanting him to be happy, but the more time drug on the more I regretted the decision to let him go. Time passed and the more it did, the more afraid I became of reaching out to him. I was happy at Seven Springs, but it wasn't the kind of happy I'd been that summer with him. I convinced myself to have faith that he was happy too. I convinced myself that he'd moved on. He'd probably remarried and he and Josh would have forgotten our summer together by now. As I lay in bed and ran my fingers over the words on the page, over the outline of his jaw in the photograph, I prayed they hadn't moved on. Of course I still wanted him to be happy, but I really hoped he wasn't as happy as he could be with me.

I wanted to call Millie right then and had it not been after midnight, and if she didn't have two little girls that I'd wake if I called, I would have dialed her up. I would have told her I wanted to go find him right then. I wanted to throw all caution to the wind because I wanted him back. Pride, consequences and whatever other excuses I'd used in the past that kept me too afraid to reach out to him be damned! I wanted him back, but most of all I wanted to know for sure if I'd done the right thing. Had I sacrificed my happiness for his? Was he happy? He looked happy in the photograph, smiling and that light in his eyes shown through, even in black and white. Was that just an act? I had to know.

I tossed and turned all night. I dreamed of Jack and he was waiting for me under the wedding tree. I awoke to memories of the dream so vivid that I cried when I realized it was only a dream. I'd let him go that summer, but I'd never really let him go. I'd never stopped hoping that he would find me. I loved my life at Seven Springs and I really had found myself here, but this would never be home. Home was Santa Rosa Beach, Florida. Home was where Jack was.

Like clockwork, Millie arrived to pick me up that morning right on time.

"Are you ready?" She asked finding me picking through the front page article about the tournament.

"As ready as I'll ever be," I shrugged, tossing the paper down on the office desk.

"You know you can do anything you set your mind to, right?" This wasn't the first time Millie had been the driving force behind me. If it weren't for her, I might have spent the rest of my life hiding out in my mother's guest room and not getting out of my pajamas for days on end.

"You seem to have more faith in my abilities than I do."

"Are you kidding me? You've got seduction written all over you!"

Completely embarrassed, I covered my face.

"Oh stop it. Like you don't know you're gorgeous." Millie started out the door leaving me standing there. Things like that were easy for her to say. When Millie entered a room, she owned it. When I entered a room, I kind of hoped no one would notice me. Millie was a firecracker and I was a wallflower. We made great friends, but personality wise, we were vastly different.

"Come on, Ugly Duckling," she called back to me. "Grab your purse and let's go."

We pulled out of the Seven Springs parking lot at 11:30 a.m. The tournament was already underway, but we weren't exactly going to watch golf so there was no reason for us to have been there when the gates opened.

If heartbeats were measured at miles per hour, my heart would have won any race against Millie's Corvette. It nearly beat out of my chest the entire way to Augusta and picked up speed the closer we got to the course. I could feel my insides starting to shake a little as we parked the car.

I shut the car door, but was reluctant to let go of the handle. I looked over the top of the car at Millie. "Maybe this wasn't a good idea."

"We're here. This is happening," Millie insisted.

"I'm not like you." I shook my head and tried not to let tears spring up, nervous tears.

"How's that?" Millie was taken aback.

"Confident."

"Then do what everyone does, what I do," Millie replied.

I had no idea what she meant. "What?"

"Fake it!" Millie held her head up, put her shoulders back and strutted around the car. Once face to face with me she repeated herself. "Fake it. Stand up straight, chin up, shoulders back and think positively."

Millie took me by the hand and we started toward the clubhouse. Along the way, she corrected me about a fundamental character flaw that I had.

"You seem to be under the impression that you're not good enough for the almighty Senator Jack Belgrave or you won't fit in his family or some craziness like that. It's called low self-esteem and you need to get over it. Just so you know, from what you've told me over the years about him, you're the only one who's ever thought you weren't good enough."

Millie and I walked the grounds, knowing he could have been anywhere and even if we found him it might take some real effort to get close to him. Not before walking the length of five fairways did we finally give up and ask one of the attendants which hole Jack might be on.

"Fourteen," the man in the green jacket replied.

"Thank you." Millie batted her eyes and the man went all starry eyed and would have given her the keys to the kingdom if she'd asked.

I knew I was pretty, but where I thought my looks were a burden, Millie didn't. She used hers to her advantage.

By the time we walked all the way to the fourteenth, Jack had moved on. We found him squaring up to pitch it to the green from the edge of a water hazard on the fifteenth. My heart jumped when I saw him.

"Wow! Look at those arms," she commented as he came around with his swing.

Jack looked better than I remembered. The sight of him warranted me fanning myself. The photograph in the paper hadn't done him justice.

Millie took my hand and we tried to get closer, but it was no use.

"I have an idea." Millie turned from the crowd and I followed. "We'll go to the next tee and wait there. We'll beat everyone else there and get a front row seat, you might say."

"Okay." With my legs shaking and my stomach flipping, I followed her eagerly.

I had momentarily forgotten that Millie and Gabe used to work at a golf course. That was actually where they met. Millie gave instructions as we approached the tee. "When he starts to swing the entire crowd is going to go silent and when they do, you say his name as sweetly as you ever had. Say it loud enough for him to hear you, but not loud enough to make a scene. I mean, don't say it like yelling 'Fore!' As soon as you do, slink back into the crowd. Don't let him see you, not yet."

"Alright." I prayed I could keep my nerves in check long enough that I could say his name. I also prayed that it didn't come out like a hiccup or like spitting out onions or anything. I walked the rest of the way to the tee box crossing my fingers and saying silent prayers.

It wasn't too terribly long and the moment was upon me. Jack was no farther than ten feet away from me. I was sweating and my hands were so clammy that I nearly dropped my clutch. He pulled back after a couple of practice swings and was about to let rip with the real thing when Millie prodded me in the side.

"Senator Belgrave," came out of my mouth just above a whisper.

Millie pulled me around in front of her and shoved me through the crowd. I was busy saying excuse me to everyone letting us pass as Millie kept pushing.

"Yes!" Millie let out, straining to keep her excitement contained.

"What?"

"He took the bait!"

"I thought you said, 'Don't look back.'"

"Yeah, but I didn't say I wouldn't look." I could tell she almost added, "Duh," to the end of that sentence. Instead she added with glee, "His head is spinning. He's looking for you."

All of this happened in seconds and in those seconds a loud thud reverberated through the wind. Millie started laughing.

"What is it?"

"He pulled his head out when you said his name and just about shanked it. He hit the tree!" she continued giggling. "We've got him right where we want him."

The rest of Millie's plan was to wait and catch him at the end of the tournament, but the plans changed. Millie watched him. Jack was scanning the crowd.

"He's going to the ropes, come on."

"Huh?"

"He's meeting and greeting folks in the crowd. Here's your chance." Around the side of the fairway Millie led picking up the pace as if we were going to a fire.

We overshot where Jack was shaking hands and talking to folks by about ten yards. Millie had me make my way to the front and by the time I did, Jack was there. He was discussing local restaurants with the patrons and taking recommendations. I thought this one man would never shut up about bar-b-que so I worked up my nerve and interrupted him.

"Have you ever heard of Seven Springs Inn?" I asked not distinguishing to whom my question was posed. "It's a small antique hotel outside of Avera, Georgia and you haven't lived until you've tried the pecan crusted Georgia mountain trout that the chef prepares there."

I struggled to stay focused on the bar-b-que man and that struggle was real. Jack was within arm's reach. I couldn't look at him. If I did, I wouldn't be able to hide the fact that my insides were jittering like a crackhead needing a fix. I could picture myself kissing him with no regard to who was watching.

The man sputtered on about Sconyers and I didn't think he was ever going to stop. I finally interrupted him again. "All I'm saying is if you want to step outside of your comfort zone, call me and I'll reserve you a table."

Trying not to fidget, I reached in my clutch and pulled out two of my business cards. I flipped one between my fingers to the man and followed with one to Jack, acknowledging him by name as I did. As soon as Jack took the card, I melted both emotionally and into the crowd as Millie had advised.

"Put the ball in his court," she instructed, "And then you'll know once and for all. He'll call you or he won't, and that will be the end or the new beginning."

I found Millie toward the back of the group of patrons. She'd heard and seen everything. "Smooth," she commented as we walked away from the seventeenth fairway. "You should have seen his face. You definitely left him wanting more."

It left me wanting more as well. A whole lot more. Didn't I deserve to be happy as well? Only time would tell.

The End

For Now...

Dear Reader,

I hope you enjoyed My Summer With the Senator. Although you've come to the end, there will be more. I'm not quite done with Caroline and Jack yet and I hope I've succeeded in leaving you wanting more.

While you wait for The Road to the White House, please help yourself to other titles in my catalogue:

<u>The Port Honor Series</u>
Port Honor
In Search of Honor
The Price of Honor

<u>The Wrightsboro Hunt Series</u>
When I Was Green
A Horse of a Different Color

As always, thank you so much for your time. Thank you for all that you do to help me reach my goal of becoming a successful author. From reading my books, to telling your friends about them, following and commenting on my Facebook page or leaving a review on Amazon.com, all your contributions are appreciated.

Don't forget I love hearing from you all. Please feel free to leave me reviews on Amazon.com as those are invaluable to authors, follow me on Facebook at my author page, T.S. Dawson Author, or email me directly through the contact section of my website (TSDawson.com).

Sincerely,

T.S. Dawson
And the Entire T.S. Dawson Team